The Yorkshire Moorland Mystery

J.S. Fletcher

OREON

This edition published 2022 by

OREON

an imprint of

The Oleander Press
16 Orchard Street
Cambridge
CB1 1JT

A CIP catalogue record for the book
is available from the British Library.

ISBN: 9781915475008

Cover design, typesetting & ebook: neorelix

For first news of titles, give-aways and discounts, sign up to our infrequent newsletter at: oleanderpress.com

Contents

Chapter One

WHERE IS HE?

THIS was the seventh day of the disappearance of Dr. Charles Essenheim from the Carlton Hotel in Pall Mall, and at noon on that day I, his secretary, had no more idea of his whereabouts than I had of what there is in the moon – perhaps less. Early one morning, a week previously, Dr. Essenheim had left me in our rooms, saying that he was just going round to a certain club close by and should not be away very long; he had gone and never returned, and I had had no news of him: no more news, at any rate, than that, on his arrival at that club, the hall-porter had handed him two telegrams which had been delivered there a few minutes before he walked in. Dr. Essenheim had read their contents there and then, and, turning at once to the door, had walked out again, hailed a passing taxi-cab, and driven away. Where he went in that cab nobody knew; that he had gone off in it I ascertained later in the morning when I called at the club to tell him that a most important client was awaiting his return to the hotel. And – to repeat myself – I never heard one word of him from then until shortly after noon on that seventh day of his strange disappearance. Then I did hear something, resultant on the arrival at the Carlton of Dr. Essenheim's

1

nephew, Frank Essenheim, newly come from America to join his uncle in England.

Before I say what that something was, I had better set down what I knew of Dr. Essenheim up to then, and how I came to know him at all. All this was just after the winding-up of the Great War. I had recently been demobilized, and was rather badly in need of employment. One morning I saw in the personal column of *The Times* an advertisement to the effect that an American gentleman, temporarily resident in London, required the services, for the time of his stay, of a well-educated young man as secretary. Not being conscious of any remarkable proficiency in education, I had very little hope of securing this position; but I replied to the advertisement, and within a few hours got a note from Dr. Essenheim, asking me to call at his hotel. Happening to open the note at the time a friend was with me who knew more about things in general than I did, I handed it to him, asking him if he knew anything of the man whose signature appeared at its foot. He showed instant appreciation.

"Essenheim?" he exclaimed. "Why, of course! One of the most famous book-collectors and authority on books living – there's only one bigger, and that, perhaps, is a matter of opinion. Oh, yes – Essenheim's well known. Comes over here regularly and buys up all the rare stuff he can lay hands on – spends piles of money. You go and see him just now that'll be a job worth having."

I went off to the Carlton there and then, but in fear and trembling, for I knew nothing about books – in that way, at any rate, and I dreaded an interview with a man who was doubtless a high-brow of the first quality. I expected to find – but I scarcely knew what. What I did find was a smartly-dressed, scrupulously groomed, brisk-mannered gentleman of middle age, of what I should have set down as the English country squire type, who put me at my ease in five minutes, and within ten he had engaged me on terms which I considered generous and handsome. An hour later I and my belongings were back at the hotel and safely housed, and my new master and I were improving our acquaintance over the luncheon-table.

That was a fortnight before Dr. Essenheim's disappearance. During that fortnight I learned a good deal about him. There is no need to go into detail here, but what chiefly struck me about Dr. Essenheim was – first, that his knowledge of what I will call the old book world seemed to me to be nothing less than uncanny; second, that he was the quickest hand at a bargain that I had ever known; and third, that he appeared to be in command of an inexhaustible purse. Nothing very eventful occurred during those two weeks; nothing, I mean, that seemed to be eventful to Dr. Essenheim. People came to his suite of rooms at the hotel, with books; sometimes he bought, sometimes he didn't; once or twice he attended sales, where his method of out-bidding anybody for anything that he was determined to have sometimes took my breath away; now and then he made a journey into the country and came back with a shabby-looking volume in his pocket for which he had given more than its weight in gold. At the time of his disappearance he was almost due in Paris, whither I was to accompany him; we were going from Paris into Germany, and thence to Italy, and after that back to London. All that came to an end the morning he walked out of our rooms with the remark that he was just going round to the Moretus Club and should not be very long away. Then for a whole week I waited, and wondered what his absence meant. About half-past twelve, noon, of the seventh day there walked into our rooms, where I was doing what I could with the accumulating correspondence, a smart, alert-looking young man, who announced himself as Frank Essenheim, and demanded his uncle. I had to tell him what he had already been told by the hotel people, supplementing it with information of my own. He looked at me wonderingly.

"But why haven't you made enquiries?" he asked. "Seven clear days!"

"The answer to that," I replied, "is that the management here, the members of which have known Dr. Essenheim for many years and are well acquainted with his habits, tell me that there is nothing whatever that is either strange or remarkable about his absence. They say that they have often known him to walk out without saying a word as to where he was going and remain away for several days and return then without a word as to where he had been. Step out, you understand, as if he were going next door – leaving these rooms just as they are."

"What! With all his valuable acquisitions unguarded?" he exclaimed.

"They are all in there," I said, pointing to a safe in the corner. "He has the key, of course."

He looked at me meditatively for a minute or so in silence.

"They didn't tell me your name, downstairs," he said at last.

"My name's Mannering," I replied. "James Mannering."

"Ex-army man, I reckon?" he suggested. "I thought so! Well, look here – I'm not satisfied about this business. You see, Uncle Charles expected me yesterday, and I ought to have been here – should have been here but for exceptionally bad weather. Instead of getting into Southampton yesterday afternoon, we didn't berth till nine o'clock this morning. Now if Uncle Charles isn't here to meet me, it means that – well, in my opinion, it means that something's wrong! Because it was of the highest importance that he should see me as soon as possible after I struck England. We've got to do something."

"What can we do?" I asked. "I've no clue whatever to his whereabouts."

"Do you know the name and address of his solicitor, and the name of his banker?" he enquired. "I don't!"

"His solicitor is Mr. Heddleston, in Bedford Row," I replied. "His London bankers are Bickford, Burgess & Co., a private bank in the City – Lombard Street."

"Come on!" he said, making for the door. "The solicitor first. Let's hear if he knows anything."

We went out into the Haymarket, chartered a taxi-cab, and drove along to Bedford Row. Mr. Heddleston, a man of about Dr. Essenheim's own age, who evidently knew him intimately, smiled when he learned the object of our visit. It was easy to see that he shared the opinion of the hotel people and saw nothing unusual in Dr. Essenheim's absence.

"But I tell you he was expecting me last night!" persisted Frank. "I say that if all was right with him, he'd have been in the hotel to receive me."

Mr. Heddleston became serious – or more serious than he had been.

"Well, I know nothing of him," he said. "He hasn't been here for at least a fortnight. Try his bankers. Find out if any cheque or cheques of his have been presented during the last day or two."

We went down to Lombard Street then, and were speedily admitted to the presence of the manager of Bickford, Burgess & Co. He, like Mr. Heddleston, shook his head at our first question.

"I don't think Dr. Essenheim has been here lately," he replied. "He doesn't often come here, but when he does, he usually drops in on me – we are old friends and fellow-bibliophiles. But I will make enquiry."

He went out – to return within a few minutes.

"Dr. Essenheim was here just a week ago," he said. "He came in one morning to cash a cheque, and was in a hurry. That's why he didn't see me that time. Exactly a week ago – the 21st October, to be precise. This, of course, is the 28th."

"What time was it when he called here?" I asked.

"About noon – the cashier said," replied the manager.

"He left me at the Carlton at a quarter to eleven," I remarked. "He must have driven here from the Moretus Club."

"You say he came to cash a cheque," said Frank. "May I know for how much, and in what form he took the money?"

The manager disappeared again. This time he was longer away, and when he returned he came fingering a slip of paper.

"Dr. Essenheim cashed a cheque made out to himself," he said. "The amount was for five thousand pounds, and he took the money in fifty notes of a hundred pounds each. Here are the numbers of the notes if you wish for them."

"Any cheques of his cashed since then?" enquired Frank.

The manager went out for the third time. He came back carrying a cheque.

"This was cashed yesterday," he reported.

"It is, you see, for two thousand pounds, and is made payable to bearer. It was presented by a lady, who took the money in Bank of England notes. We have the numbers of those too."

Frank Essenheim considered matters in silence for a moment or two.

"Nothing out of the common in all this, I suppose?" he said at last.

"Nothing!" replied the manager. "Nothing at all! Dr. Essenheim always keeps a big balance here – what some businessmen would regard as a very big balance. When he is in town on one of his book-buying visits, he frequently draws out large sums in cash: I have heard him say, more than once, that some of the people he buys from privately prefer cash payments to payments by cheque. There is nothing unusual either about that cheque – the one presented by the lady. We frequently cash cheques of Dr. Essenheim's made payable to bearer for bigger amounts than that. Dr. Essenheim's dealings, as you are both probably aware, are on a princely scale!"

"I know!" assented Frank. He stood, apparently thinking, for another spell of silence, and then picked up his hat. "Then you know nothing of his whereabouts?" he said.

"Nothing whatever!" replied the manager. "But considering that he called here the morning he left his hotel and took five thousand pounds away in notes, I have an idea. I should say he went off somewhere to buy something!"

"Yes – but he should have been back last night, anyway, to meet me," persisted Frank.

"That's the ugly fact that I don't like. He knew how important it was that he should see me as soon as I landed."

We went away, and, after consultation as to our next move, decided to go back to Heddleston's office and tell him the result of our enquiries, and hailing the first available taxi-cab, we drove back to Bedford Row. Heddleston, his clerks said, was still out at lunch, but was expected back at any moment; we waited for him in his room. Presently he came in, and at sight of us he gave a palpable start; it was evident we were in his thoughts.

"I was just going to 'phone you," he said, and held up a newspaper which he carried in his left hand. "There is something in this early edition which – but you had better read it for yourselves. After all, it mayn't be – "

He paused abruptly at that, and, spreading the newspaper on his desk before us, silently pointed to a paragraph headed

Startling Discovery on a Yorkshire Moor. Standing side by side we read what followed.

KIRKENMORE, YORKSHIRE,
Monday Morning

A startling discovery, now actively engaging the attention of the local police, was made on the moors near here at an early hour this morning, when a man named Hopkinson, employed as a shepherd at a moorland farm, found, wedged in a crevice at the foot of Harlesden Scar, a mass of precipitous rock situate in the wild country between Kirkenmore and Rievesley, the dead body of a well-dressed man, which had evidently lain there for some days. Hopkinson at once communicated with the nearest village constable, and the body was removed to the mortuary at Kirkenmore, where it now lies. The authorities are very reticent about the matter, but as there are no papers in the clothing which give any clue to the identity of the deceased, they have requested the Press to make it known that the body is that of a man of apparently forty-five to fifty years of age, very well and smartly dressed in a medium-grey lounge suit and inexpensive linen and underwear. The face is clean-shaven, except for a small military moustache, lightly grey; a little above the left elbow there is a birthmark in the shape of a large brown mole. In one of the inner pockets of the lounge jacket was found a small book, presumably of value, and printed at Amsterdam in 1647. Anyone recognising the dead man from these particulars should communicate at once with the Superintendent of Police at Kirkenmore.

Frank Essenheim read through this without sign or sound. But there was meaning enough in his voice when he looked up and turned quietly to Heddleston and myself.

"This Kirkenmore?" he said in calm, level tones. "Now, how soon can we get there?"

Chapter Two

FOUND DEAD!

HEDDLESTON reached for a Bradshaw that lay on a corner of his desk, shaking his head as he began to turn over its pages.

"I don't know that part of the country," he said. "Yorkshire is a big country – "

"I know Kirkenmore," said I. "I have been there often. It is a very small market town on the North York Moors, in a very wild and lonely stretch of country, and about thirty miles north-east of York. You get to it from King's Cross."

"Through York, of course," remarked Heddleson. "Well, there's an express from King's Cross at 4 o'clock which reaches York at 8.6." He glanced at the clock on his mantelpiece. "It's now a quarter-past three," he went on. "Three-quarters of an hour doesn't give much time, but – "

"I'm going on that train," said Frank. "Where are we now in relation to King's Cross?"

"Practically close by," replied Heddleston. He put down the railway guide and glanced at an open diary which lay on his desk. "I think I had better go with you," he continued. "You may want legal advice. And," he added, hesitatingly, "I'm afraid, from this description, that this is Dr. Essenheim! Well – no use speculating or wondering till we get there! Mr.

Mannering – do you know of any reason why Dr. Essenheim should have gone down to Yorkshire?"

"None!" I replied. "I'm quite sure he had no such journey in view when he went out of our rooms at the Carlton a week ago."

"Nothing in his correspondence that referred to such a journey?"

"Nothing! He had appointments at the hotel for that day – one very important appointment. He had engagements for the next day too – and on the third he was to have attended a sale in which he was keenly interested."

"You say he received two telegrams when he went into the Moretus Club that morning? Well, it's obvious that there must have been something in one or the other that sent him off there and then – "

"We haven't told you the result of our enquiry at the bank," I said, interrupting him.

"Dr. Essenheim appears to have driven straight from the Moretus Club to the bank, where he drew five thousand pounds in Bank of England notes of a hundred pounds each. He gave the bank people to understand that he was in a hurry. Usually when he called there on any business he stopped and had a chat with the manager."

"Must have been some urgent call in one of those wires," muttered Heddleston. "Well – did you learn anything else there? Any cheques cashed during the last day or two which would give any idea as to his whereabouts?"

"There was a bearer cheque for two thousand pounds cashed there yesterday by a lady – quite a usual transaction, according to the manager," I replied.

"Didn't hear of any with a country endorsement?" he asked.

"No; that was all we heard. The manager, like the hotel people, didn't seem to attach any great importance to the facts we put before him."

Heddleston turned and, picking up a small suitcase that lay in a corner, snapped it open for an instant and glanced into it.

"Always keep this ready packed up for an emergency," he remarked. "But you two – can you manage? There's no time to get things from your hotel. All right? – well, money?"

"I've plenty of money on me for all three," said Frank. "Let's get that train."

"Wait a moment," said Heddleston. He went into another room and came back in a minute or two stuffing a handful of paper money into a note-case. "Now," he continued, picking up his suitcase, "come on! I wish we hadn't all these hours to wait."

We said little on our way to King's Cross, and perhaps less in the train. There was a restaurant car and there was afternoon tea and two hours later there was dinner: we ate and drank mostly in a gloomy silence. For, as Heddleston had said, there was no good to be got out of mere speculation. Nevertheless, I myself spent most of that journey, not in speculating and wondering, to be sure, but in trying to recall anything in Dr. Essenheim's correspondence or conversation during the time I had been in his service which could suggest a reason for any visit to Yorkshire. And I could think of nothing.

There was no train from York to Kirkenmore that night; nothing before twelve minutes to eight next morning. Heddleston, I think, would have been glad enough to turn into the Station Hotel, and so should I, but such a course had no place in Frank Essenheim's thoughts, and within a quarter of an hour of our stepping out of the express we were in a fast car, chartered after critical inspection, and off northward again. A little before half-past nine we drew up at the police station in Kirkenmore and were presently ushered into the presence of a big, somewhat stolid-faced man in uniform whom the policeman on duty addressed as Super-intendent Calvert. We had wired to the Kirkenmore police before leaving London, and as soon as Calvert saw us he sent out a man with two messages.

"I fancied you'd come on by car from York, gentlemen," he said, offering us seats near the fire, "and I've asked Dr. Belliss, our police-surgeon, and Mr. Whittaker, the landlord of the hotel, to be in readiness to come across as soon as you arrived – they'll be here presently. You think this gentleman is the one you've missed?"

"That can be decided in a moment, Superintendent," said Heddleston. "The body is, I understand, in your mortuary. Then – you had better take me there. Mr. Essenheim," he continued, turning to Frank, "You remain here – I can do all that is necessary at present."

Frank assented to this by a silent nod: he understood the solicitor's meaning. And Heddleston and Calvert went out and within five minutes were back again. Heddleston gave us a nod and a word.

"Yes!"

"No doubt in any way?" asked Frank quietly.

"None!" replied Heddleston. He turned to Calvert. "Just tell us what you can," he said.

"We know nothing beyond what we read in an early edition of one of the London evening papers. He was found by a man crossing the moors, eh?"

"That's so, sir," replied Calvert. "To be particular, it was the man's dog that made the discovery. After it had been made, the man, Hopkinson, a shepherd, fetched the nearest village constable and he communicated with me, and I went out there with Dr. Belliss, who'll be here presently. The body was wedged in a crevice at the foot of a pile of rocks known here as Harlesden Crag, in a very wild and lonely bit of country, and our first idea was that the poor gentleman was a tourist who had missed his way and walked over the top – an accident, you understand – ”

“Isn't it your idea, now?” interrupted Frank.

“No, sir – and you'll know why presently,” replied Calvert. “I was going to say that we made an examination of the clothing there and then, before removing the body here. There was nothing on it – I mean in the way of money, valuables, papers, letters – anything by which it could be identified. I could see there'd been rings on both hands – one on each third finger – but they were gone. All that we did find was – this.”

He turned to his desk, unlocked a drawer, and silently produced and laid before us a small volume, some five inches by three in size, bound in its original leather.

“It was in a hip-pocket,” added Calvert. “As if it had been valuable. Perhaps it is – I have no knowledge of such things.”

Heddleston picked up the book and held it towards me.

“Do you know anything of it?” he asked.

“No!” I replied. “Never seen it before. It was not in his possession when he left town, I'm certain.”

Heddleston handed the book back.

“Well?” he enquired. “What else, Superintendent? The body had been robbed? But – the cause of death? Have you formed any theory – any conclusion?”

Calvert gave us a covert look. He shook his head.

“I have, sir! The gentleman was murdered!” he answered. “Not a doubt of it!”

There was a moment's silence. Then Frank spoke – more quietly than ever.

“You have reason for saying that.”

"I have, sir!" replied Calvert. "I – but I think those two gentlemen I sent for are here – Dr. Belliss and Mr. Whittaker. Dr. Belliss can answer your question, sir, better than I can."

The two men he spoke of were ushered in just then. Dr. Belliss, a grave, elderly man, shook his head when Calvert told him what Frank had just inquired.

"I do not think there can be the least doubt that the unfortunate gentleman was the victim of a savage and a cowardly attack!" he said. "In my opinion, based on a most careful examination – and it is supported by two other medical men who have been here during the day – he was struck two terrible blows on the head with a heavy, blunt weapon, either of which blows was sufficient to cause instant death, and, after being robbed of whatever was on him, was thrown over the top of the pile of rocks at the foot of which the body was found. I say – there is no doubt!"

Once more there was silence. Calvert broke it.

"Up to now, sir," he said, glancing at Heddleston, "we don't know who the deceased gentleman is? From the signature to your telegram to us, I take you to be Mr. Heddleston, a London solicitor."

"I was the dead man's solicitor," replied Heddleston. "And he was Dr. Charles Essenheim, an American gentleman who was famous throughout the world as a great book-collector. This young gentleman is his nephew, Mr. Frank Essenheim; the other is Captain Mannering, Dr. Essenheim's secretary. Dr. Essenheim, as Captain Mannering can tell you, left the Carlton Hotel in London, hurriedly, a week ago, did not return and has never been heard of by any of us until now."

Calvert was making a note in a book; he turned from it to Heddleston.

"A wealthy gentleman, sir?" he asked.

"Yes!" replied Heddleston, laconically. "He was very wealthy."

"Likely to have much money on him, sir?"

"I dare say he had plenty of money on him!"

"Expensive things in the way of watch, chain, rings too, eh?" suggested Calvert.

"No doubt!" agreed Heddleston. "And just before leaving town, evidently preparatory to coming into this neighbourhood, he drew five thousand pounds from his bank, in Bank of England notes of a hundred pounds each. Whether he had those notes on him at the time of what appears to have been his murder – "

"Decided case of murder!" murmured Dr. Belliss. "Not one doubt of it!"

"I, of course, can't say," concluded Heddleston. "At present, Superintendent, what we should like to get is some information about Dr. Essenheim's being here at all, for Captain Mannering, who knew all his affairs, knows nothing about his having any appointment hereabouts."

Calvert turned to the man who had come in with the doctor.

"Mr. Whittaker can tell you all there is to tell, sir," he said. "Mr. Whittaker's the landlord of the Muzzled Ox. This poor gentleman – Dr. Essenheim is the name? – stayed there one night last week."

We all turned on Whittaker – a quiet-looking man who cleared his throat with a nervous cough.

"One night, only, gentlemen," he said. "Monday night, it was – the 21st October, which to be sure, this is Monday the 28th – a week ago. He came in latish – in a car or a taxi-cab – I think he said he'd driven from York. He wanted supper and a room, and was particular about the room. We did our best for him – fire in his room and all that. He had supper and went to his room soon afterwards. I didn't see much of him after he'd once come, and I only just had a glimpse of him next morning. He had breakfast at nine o'clock, paid his bill, and went out. And, of course, never returned."

"Never returned, eh?" said Heddleston.

"No, sir – he never returned," replied Whittaker. "And we never had his name – he didn't put it in the visitors' book when he arrived, and my missus forgot to ask him to do so before he went off next morning."

"Do you know where he went?" asked Heddleston.

"Superintendent Calvert there has asked me that, sir," said Whittaker. "No, I do not! But our ostler, who is the only man I know of who seems to have seen him after he left the front door, says that he saw him turn the corner into the road to Rievesley."

"Where is Rievesley? – and what is it – town or village?" continued Heddleston.

"Small town, like this, sir," replied Whittaker. "About five miles away."

"Are there any villages between here and Rievesley?"

"Two or three, sir."

"We've been making inquiries in all of them during the day, Mr. Heddleston," remarked Calvert. "We've failed to discover anything. Up to now I haven't been able to get a scrap of information about this gentleman from the time he was seen turning into the Rievesley road to the finding of his body this morning. Where he went to when he left the Muzzled Ox, I can't make out!"

Heddleston turned to Dr. Belliss.

"In your opinion, Doctor, how long had Dr. Essenheim been dead when you examined the body?" he asked. "Can you say?"

Dr. Belliss appeared to have no hesitation in saying.

"Five or six days," he answered promptly. "Probably six."

There was no more to be said or done that night. We went with Whittaker to the Muzzled Ox, a quaint, old-fashioned hostelry, and retired to get what rest we could before entering on the next day's labours. It was a long time before I could get to sleep. The question was there, always there: "What had brought Dr. Essenheim to Yorkshire?"

Chapter Three

THE WIRE FROM LONDON

ALTHOUGH my bed was comfortable enough, I did but poorly in it, turning about wakefully for the greater part of the night, and as soon as it grew fairly light in the morning I was glad to get up, dress, and make my way downstairs. There was no one about, but hearing a sound in the back regions of the house I penetrated to a big kitchen, in which I found a man who was evidently coaxing a kettle to boil on a newly-lighted fire. He showed no surprise at my appearance and bade me a civil good morning.

"You the boots?" I enquired, after wishing him the same.

"Sort of a bit of everything, I am, sir," he answered with a whimsical smile. "Boots, knives, ostler, and whatnot. What you'd call an odd-job man, sir. Can I get you a cup of tea, now?"

That was just what I wanted, and I sat down near the fire and watched him putting out cups and saucers, milk and sugar. Then I remembered something that the landlord had told us at the police station.

"Are you the man who saw the last of Dr. Essenheim?" I enquired.

"The dead gentleman, sir? I am!" he replied. "Yes, sir, I saw him last – as far as any of us is aware. Got him an early cup of tea that morning, same as I'm getting you one. He was up early, too – sat in that very chair as you're sitting in while he drank his tea, sir."

"Did he talk to you?" I asked.

"He did, sir. Wanted to know how far it was to Rievesley, and which was the road to take. And then a few more questions about the country hereabouts – what was it like – and so on."

"Pretty wild and lonely country it is about here, isn't it?" I suggested. "Nothing but moorland?"

"Moors, hills, valleys, sir – that's about it. Bit of good arable land here and there in the valleys, but for the most part good for nothing but grouse. This side – " he waved a hand northward – "you can go for miles and miles and scarce see a house – very solitary neighbourhood, sir."

"Where is the place at which the body was found?" I asked.

"Harlesden Scar, sir? About a mile and a half north-by-west. Great pile of rocks on the hillside overlooking this valley. Dangerous spot, that, sir."

"How should he come by there?" I inquired.

"Well, sir, we've all had a lot of talk about that point. What I think is that somebody showed the poor gentleman a near cut across the moors by a path that would take him right across the top of the Scar. And, as he was murdered, according to the doctors, I reckon whoever did it attacked him there, and after going through his pockets flung the body over the rocks. But you'll no doubt see the place for yourself, sir – ugly place to fall over, is that. Your tea, sir."

I drank the tea and then went out into the little town – a place of one main street with another turning off it.

It was a raw autumn morning; scarcely anybody seemed to be stirring; the hills outside were swathed in circling mists; the trees had already lost their leaves, and everything looked so cheerless that I began to regret the kitchen fire. And as I strolled about I wondered again and yet again – whatever was it that had brought Dr. Essenheim to this out-of-the-way place and to his death?

Heddleston, Frank Essenheim, and I went round to the police station as soon as we had breakfasted; there were arrangements to be made about the opening of the inquest and the removal of the body for burial in London. But within an hour we were all in Calvert's car and on our way to the scene of the murder. Our route lay for only a little way along the high road between Kirkenmore and Rievesley; it quickly deviated into a moorland track which soon brought us in sight of Harlesden Scar and eventually led to the top of it. And here we got out and looked round us. Had the occasion been other than it was, I should have delighted in the scene which opened before us. The early morning mists had cleared away under the warmth of the autumn sun, and from the top of the Scar we could look across country in every direction and over what appeared to be limitless prospects. Southward we could discern the towers of the great minster at York; westward, the long blue-grey line of the Pennine Range, separating Yorkshire from Lancashire; eastward and northward the moors and hills stretched as far as the eye could reach in what seemed a houseless solitude. Looking around more closely one could discern, here and there, a wisp of curling smoke that denoted the presence of a lonely farmstead; somewhat to our west a congregation of such wisps and the spire of a church denoted the presence of a town or village. To this Calvert at once pointed.

"That's Rievesley!" he said. "There, where there's smoke hanging over the roofs, and where you see the spire. Now, that's what beats me. If your friend went to Rievesley from Kirkenmore in the morning, as he presumably did, and by the highroad that leads straight from one place to the other, why should he come back by way of this Harlesden Scar? It's true there's a series of by-paths that cut across the moors between the two places – here it is, crossing, do you see, the top of the Scar – but it's no nearer, and it's bad walking. And if he took it at night, all the more wonder. Besides, how should he, a stranger, know of it? Do any of you gentlemen know if he'd ever been in these parts before?"

None of us knew. But Heddleston voiced what we all three felt.

"Dr. Essenheim, Superintendent, may have chosen this moorland path for its solitude and scenery," he said. "Somebody told him of it, no doubt. But there are two or three things that occur to me. He may – we'll say he did ask his way to Rievesley, but what he really wanted may have been a house near Rievesley. You have no proof, have you, that he was seen in Rievesley?"

"Haven't heard that he was, sir," replied Calvert. "We've never heard a word about him beyond what you've heard of. All we know is that his body was found – here!"

"Show us just where," said Heddleston.

Calvert led us to the very edge of the Scar and pointed downward to the broken masses of rock at its foot. There was a sheer, precipitous drop there, of some hundred and fifty to two hundred feet.

"It was found," he said, "in that crevice that you see down there – that one with the hawthorn bush growing out of it. Firmly wedged in, it was – and of course, there'd been damage done by the fall. But then, according to the doctor, that wasn't the cause of death. I work it out that he was attacked up here, on the path, stunned, perhaps killed at once, and that when the murderer – "

"Or murderers!" interjected Heddleston.

"Quite right, sir; I'm of that opinion myself," assented Calvert. "When they'd done with him, they carried the body to the edge here and flung it over. Where the actual assault took place there's nothing to show. We examined every inch of the top here yesterday, and we found no footmarks. But then, as you see, this turf is short, springy, and resilient, as they say, and it doesn't readily take impressions."

Heddleston nodded, and going back to the path, which, in reality, was nothing whatever but a mere sheep-track, looked about him.

"I see no signs of any struggle hereabouts," he remarked. "But then, how do we know that the murder took place here at all? It may have taken place elsewhere, and the murderers may have brought the body here afterwards."

Calvert shook his head at that.

"Aye, sir, but just look at where we're standing!" he said. "You see we're, as it were, on the very peak of – well, something like a pyramid or a sugar-loaf; not quite so steep perhaps, but pretty steep for all that, and on every side. It would have been a stiff job for anybody to carry a dead man up to the top of this Scar, just to fling it over the edge. What is most surprising, in my mind, is that the poor gentleman should ever have been up here at all!"

"There's nothing surprising in it!" observed Frank curtly. "He was brought up here – to see the view. Who brought him?"

Nobody attempted an answer to that question. For a minute or two we all stood in silence, staring at the rocks beneath. Then Heddleston, looking round, pointed in the direction of Rievesley.

"What house is that down there in the valley?" he asked. "That big, solitary place amongst the trees?"

Looking in the direction indicated, I noticed, for the first time, the roofs and chimneys of a square mansion of considerable size which lay in a depression half a mile away to the west and was half hidden by a ring of elm and beech. Heddleston was right in calling it solitary; there was not another house nor even a cottage near it.

"That's Mr. Lomas' place, sir," replied Calvert. "Squire Lomas, we call him hereabouts. Harlesden Hall, it's called. Old family, that, sir, but fallen on evil times this last generation or two. All the land round here used to belong to that family, but they've gradually parted with it until there's next to nothing left but the house itself, and it's said that it's falling into wrack and ruin through neglect. Horse-racing and gambling, gentlemen – that's the explanation."

Heddleston, while listening to this, was, closely examining the surroundings of Harlesden Hall through a pair of field-glasses which I had seen him borrow from the landlord of the hotel before we set out. He turned to Calvert.

"It seems to me," he said, "that this path leads past that house. If Dr. Essenheim came by it from Rievesley or thereabouts, he would pass the house, wouldn't he? Very good – then I purpose that we go down there and make enquiry. But perhaps you've been there already, Superintendent?"

"No, sir – at least, I haven't," replied Calvert. "But there were two of my men – two constables, making enquiries all round about here yesterday, and I daresay they were there. If they were, they said nothing to me. I think that if Mr. Lomas knew anything or had heard anything he'd have communicated with us before now – the news of the discovery spread pretty quickly yesterday morning. However, we can walk down there."

We went down the hillside, crossed the stretch of moorland, always following the path, and soon came to the high wall which shut in Harlesden Hall, a solitude in itself, from the solitude around it. It needed but one glance to show us that Calvert's story of fallen fortunes was true enough. The fine old ironwork of the entrance gates was rusting to decay; the lodge was untenanted; the pleasure grounds in front of the house were untended and choked with weeds; grass grew on the drives and paths. The house itself, a fine example of the English Later Renaissance, looked as if it had been untenanted for years: blinds and shutters were drawn in every window, and a glance at the chimneys showed them smokeless. And when we rang the bell of the front door and heard its reverberating sound somewhere far off inside the house there was no reply, and a second and a third summons produced no other result.

Then, suddenly, from round a corner of the house appeared a man. He was neither footman nor groom nor gardener, but suggested something of all three: a queer, unkempt, uncertain-age figure that came to a halt as soon as he saw us and stood eyeing us with dislike and suspicion. Before we could address any question to him he snapped out a word or two.

"He isn't at home!"

"Mr. Lomas?" said Calvert. "Not at home, eh? Where is he, then?"

"Can't say! Been away nigh on a week. Nobody's at home but me."

"When will Mr. Lomas be back?" asked Calvert. "Don't know? Where is he? – do you know that."

But the man had turned on his heel and was disappearing round the corner from which he had emerged. Calvert shook his head.

"I've heard of that chap!" he said. "He's all the servant Mr. Lomas keeps nowadays. Sort of general factotum. We shall get nothing out of him. We'd better get back to Kirkenmore, gentlemen, and see if any news has come in there."

"And then, I think, go on to Rievesley," said Heddleston. "Presuming, from what the ostler at the hotel said, that Dr. Essenheim went to Rievesley on the morning after his arrival, we ought to be able to get some news of him there."

"Aye, sir! – if he went there," replied Calvert. "But we don't know that he did. There are one or two places between the two towns; he may have been making for one of those. I suppose," he added, glancing from one to the other of us, "I suppose none of you gentlemen know what your friend came here for ?"

"We don't know!" said Heddleston. "But there is one thing certain: it would be to see somebody. Just before he left London Dr. Essenheim received two telegrams; we shall have to find out if they were sent from this neighbourhood, and by whom."

"We can begin that at our post office," remarked Calvert. "I'll see to it as soon as we're back. That would be Monday morning, the 21st. They'll soon tell me at our post office; there are not many telegrams sent off from here."

But before he had an opportunity of visiting the Kirkenmore post office, Calvert received a wire himself.

As we got out of the car in front of the police station a constable came out with a buff envelope.

"Just come, Superintendent," he said. "Not five minutes since."

Calvert tore open the cover, ran his eye over the contents, and turned to us with an exclamation of surprise.

"This is a bit astonishing!" he said. "Listen – it's from Mr. Lomas – sent from King's Cross station. 'Can tell you something about dead man and am returning by next train!' Now, what's that mean, I wonder?"

The constable was lingering close by: evidently he wished to speak. He spoke.

"There's Mr. Kershaw, landlord of the Harp and Crown at Rievesley, waiting to see you, Superintendent," he said. "He's been here some time, and he's identified the dead gentleman."

Chapter Four

THE UNKNOWN LADY

WE found Kershaw sitting by a big fire in the Superintendent's room – a big stout, comfortable man, very much wrapped up about the throat and shoulders, and wearing an old-fashioned horseman's cloak, the sort of thing with many capes and calculated to turn the sharpest wind: Heddleston said of him, later, that he was just the desirable witness the legal mind desires – stolid, un-imaginative, matter-of-fact. He gave the three strangers a shrewd, appraising glance and nodded familiarly to Calvert.

"'Morning, Superintendent," he said. "I should have been over to see you yesterday as soon as I got the news of this affair, but I've had a touch of bronchitis and had to keep indoors. This poor gentleman, now? I've seen his body, and I've identified it."

"As – what, Mr. Kershaw?" asked Calvert. "Did you know him?"

"Not from Adam – so to speak, and as regards his name," replied the landlord. "No, sir – stranger to these parts, I

29

reckon. I identify him, Superintendent, as a gentleman who spent some hours at my place one day last week. Knew him as soon as ever I saw him – his body, I mean."

"Mr. Kershaw," remarked Calvert, turning to the rest of us, "is the landlord – "

"Proprietor!" interjected Kershaw.

"Proprietor of the Harp and Crown Hotel at Rievesley," continued Calvert. "That's what he means by his place. So the dead gentleman came there, did he, Mr. Kershaw? – one day last week. What day, now?"

"Tuesday, October 22nd, sir," replied Kershaw promptly. "No mistakes about precise dates with me! That was the day, sir."

"What time did he come in?" asked Calvert.

Kershaw settled himself more firmly in his chair in the attitude of a man who has a story to tell and is going to tell it in his own way.

"The first time, Superintendent, at a minute or two after eleven o'clock," he answered. "He walked into our bar parlour: I was in there, behind the bar, myself – it was just opening time, you see. Now I reckon I know every gentleman there is in this neighbourhood of ours, and I knew he was a perfect stranger: I set him down as a visitor to one of the big houses in the district, having a walk round. When he spoke I knew he wasn't an Englishman – American, likely, or maybe a Canadian. He had a glass of my bitter ale – no finer, gentlemen, in Yorkshire! – and then asked me two questions. First, was the railway station near? Second, could he and a lady whom he was going to meet at the station have lunch at our place if they came back there? I showed him through the parlour window where the station is, and assured him that he should be accomodated with a lunch fit for the King himself at one o'clock. He laughed and said that what would do for the King would do for him, and drank off his ale and went away to the station. A very pleasant, affable gentleman! – poor fellow!"

"Well? – he came back?" suggested Calvert.

"At about a quarter-past twelve, Superintendent. Of course, I knew what train he'd been to meet – the one that gets in from York at 11.37. As it's only five minutes walk from the Harp and Crown to the station, I reckoned he'd been showing the lady round the village a bit – there's a deal of what tourists call interesting to see in Rievesley, gentlemen. I was at the door when they came in, and I showed 'em into our lounge until lunch was ready. You know our lounge, Mr. Calvert – you've been in it often enough – and how comfortable it is, and what a lot of fine old furniture, the real, genuine old stuff, I have in it – they were highly set up with it, I could see, and began looking round 'em as if they both knew something about old oak and old china and old glass, of which I possess a deal. There was nobody else came in that morning, for lunch, I mean, so they had the lounge and a grand fire all to themselves. All the same, I didn't regard 'em as lovers or sweethearts, or aught of that sort."

"Why not, Mr. Kershaw?" asked Heddleston.

"Well, sir, this poor gentleman, he wasn't exactly a chicken, though a well-preserved, good-figured man – I should ha' set him down at a good fifty. But the lady was – well, a young 'un."

"How young?" enquired Heddleston. "Really young – a girl?"

Kershaw looked across the hearth at Calvert and smiled slily.

"We call all women girls, here in Yorkshire, sir," he said. "I call my sisters and my wife's sisters girls, though they'll none of 'em see forty again! This was a young lass, sir – maybe nineteen years old – maybe a tiny bit more."

"Can you describe her?" asked Heddleston. "It's highly important that we should get a description of her at first hand."

"Well, sir, I'm not much of a hand at that! She was a very pretty young lady, I can say that – uncommon pretty. Tallish, slimmish, and – and of the fair variety. Fair hair and complexion, you understand."

"Well-dressed, Mr. Kershaw?"

"There, sir, you beat me! She would be, I'm sure: she was a lady, and a high-bred 'un. But I'm no hand at that. If I'd my wife, or our waitress here, they could tell you – women, sir, notices things that men doesn't."

"Did you talk to her at all, Mr. Kershaw? Could you tell if she was an Englishwoman?"

"I talked to the young lady a fair lot, sir, after lunch, about some rare old pewter I have in my hall. Englishwoman right enough, sir! – and as I said before, a high-bred 'un. I know 'em! – and the way they talk, too."

"Well, about her and the gentleman, now? They had lunch – in your coffee or dining-room, I suppose?"

"They had, sir – and a rare good lunch it was, that day. The piece de resistance, as I'm told the Frenchmen call the principal feature of a meal, was as prime a saddle of mutton as ever I put knife into – and I'm a rare judge of good meat! The gentleman asked me soon after they came in what we'd got for lunch; when I told him he wanted to know if I'd got some real good, tip-top claret in my cellar? I had – I have, if any of you gentlemen want to taste it – and I fetched him a bottle or two to look at – Chateaux-Lafite, gentlemen, that came out of Lord Bideswell's famous cellar – I bought twelve dozen of it at the sale of that nobleman's effects. And me and the gentleman – I could see he knew a lot about wines – saw to its being served at the proper temperature. Oh yes, we saw to things being right!"

"I'm sure you would, Mr. Kershaw," said Heddleston. "Now, you're evidently a very noticing and observant man, and you were interested in these two guests of yours, I think – "

"Certainly, sir, certainly! I'm always interested in any lady or gentleman that patronizes my establishment," said the landlord. "That's me, sir!"

"Well, did you form the impression that these two knew each other very well? Were they very friendly? – from what you saw?"

"Yes, sir! To use a Yorkshire term – which Mr. Calvert there will understand – there were as thick as thieves! Very friendly, sir – laughed and joked together and seemed highly suited with each other's society. In fact, before they left I wondered whether I shouldn't have to alter my opinion."

"To what?"

"Well, I thought, or began to think, that after all, it might be a lovers' meeting. He was a well-preserved and a good-looking man, and nowadays young ladies, I've noticed, seem to fancy middle-aged men more than young 'uns."

"You didn't see any love-making?"

"I did not, sir. To be sure, they'd opportunities. After lunch, they had coffee served in the lounge, and they had the lounge all to themselves until half-past four o'clock when they left – after a cup of tea had been taken in for the lady. No, I saw no love-making. But I'll tell you what I did see just before they went away, the lounge door being wide open and my bar-parlour door being open, too! I saw the gentleman write a cheque and hand it to the lady. She seemed mighty pleased with it, too!"

"How could you tell that?"

"By her behaviour, sir. She shook his hand in – well, you understand, as if she was – I should say, grateful. And she looked at him – ah, there was no doubt she was grateful!"

"Very interesting, Mr. Kershaw! I see you're a man of sentiment."

"Feeling, sir, feeling! I should say the gentleman had done, or was doing, the young lady some uncommon good turn in giving her that cheque. Which, I'm sure, by her manner, she appreciated. As I've said more than once, gentlemen, she was a high-bred 'un.'"

"I wish we knew who she was!" sighed Heddleston. "We shall have to find her. But now, Mr. Kershaw, what happened after the episode of the cheque? Did they leave the hotel then?"

"They did, sir. I was in the hall when they were going out. The young lady shook hands with me and said something pretty – that showed me she was a real lady and none of your imitation articles. But the gentleman said he'd be coming back in a few minutes, after he'd seen her off – he wanted to ask me a question."

"Did he come back?"

"He did, sir. He came back in twenty minutes – came into the bar-parlour to me. He gave me a very fine cigar and we had a whisky and soda together. Then he asked me if I could tell him the exact whereabouts of Harlesden Hall. He knew, he said, that it was some-where between Rievesley and Kirkenmore, and he'd gathered from a map of the district that it could be reached by a path across the moors."

"You gave him the information he wanted?"

"Yes, sir – as a matter of fact I went out with him after we'd chatted a bit, and put him on to the moorland path at the end of the town street. He shook hands, thanked me, and went off... and that was the last I saw of him until just now, when I saw him – dead!"

Although Calvert had left whatever questioning there was of Kershaw to Heddleston, he had listened with close attention to the landlord's story, and as Heddleston showed no sign of asking further questions he began to ask some of his own.

"Had you any other strangers in to lunch that day, Kershaw?" he enquired. "I know you generally have a few people in every day, Rievesley being a sort of show place. Was there anybody that day that you didn't know?"

"There was nobody else in for lunch," replied Kershaw. "It varies, you know. In summer and especially in August and the first half of September we get no end of people – sometimes our dining-room's packed out and we scarcely know where to make room. After that it tails off. Of course, we never know what we might have, and we're always provided. Businessmen come – commercials and so on. But that day there was nobody but those two. There was, however, a man, a perfect stranger to me, who came in just after lunch. He walked into the lounge first, and then crossed over into the bar parlour."

"Did he see those two – the gentleman and young lady?" asked Calvert.

"Couldn't fail – they were in the lounge, having their coffee."

"What sort of man was he?"

"I set him down for a business man – better sort of a commercial traveller. A tall, broad-shouldered, well-dressed man. He came in again later on – at the same time that the dead gentleman was in; the second time. He was there, in fact, when I was telling him the way to Harlesden Hall, but he'd left when I came back from showing the path. It struck me as a bit strange that this second man I'm talking about should still be in the town at that time, because our last train to anywhere had gone. However, I concluded he'd got a car somewhere about."

"You'll have to give us a fuller description of that second man," said Calvert. "We may want to trace him. But now here's another thing, Kershaw: Did the gentleman – you know who I mean – tell you why he was going to Harlesden Hall?"

"Not a word!"

"Not even a hint?"

"Not even that! He said nothing."

"Did he mention Mr. Lomas?"

"No! He asked and said no more than what I've told you."

"You say he went down to your station with the young lady – that would be to catch the 4.27, eh? Now, did you happen to hear where she was going? Did she drop a word, for instance, before leaving your place?"

"She didn't," replied Kershaw. "But I know where she booked for. I came on here by train this morning, and when I was at our station I asked the booking-clerk if he remembered the young lady and the gentleman with her? He did – quite well. She took a first-class ticket for York."

"Just one more question about the other man," said Heddleston, "the man you didn't know; You say he was in your bar parlour when the man who was afterwards found dead asked you about Harlesden Hall. Did he hear Dr. Essenheirn – for that, you know by now, is the name of the gentleman whose death we're enquiring about – did he hear him ask for Harlesden Hall? Did he hear him say anything about it – mention it, specifically?"

Kershaw responded to that with an emphatic nod.

"He certainly would, sir! What the dead gentleman, Dr. Essenheim you call him, said – and the man was sitting close by – was that he wished to make a call at Harlesden Hall on his way back to Kirkenmore and he understood there was a short cut to both places by a path across the moors. Yes; the other man couldn't fail to hear that."

"And you say that when you came back from showing Dr. Essenheim the way, the man had gone?"

"He'd gone!"

"It would be dark then, I suppose – or getting so?"

"Getting on, at any rate."

This was all that Kershaw could tell, and he presently went away after pressing us to look in upon him at the Harp and Crown when we went over to Rievesley. Certainly he had thrown a good deal of light on what had hitherto been a mystery. We now knew that Dr. Essenheim had had a double object in visiting this district and that Lomas, on his arrival, would probably be able to tell us exactly why he visited Harlesden Hall and what time he left it – presumably for his previous night's quarters at Kirkenmore. And about five o'clock that afternoon Calvert sent over to the Muzzled Ox to tell us that Lomas had just arrived; we went across to the police station at once and found him with the Superintendent – a man of about thirty years of age, good-looking, but having a suspicion of dissipation about him, who silently examined all three of us as if wishing to know his company before opening his lips. He merely nodded when Calvert introduced us, and I saw at once that he had the true countryman's dislike of strangers. But Calvert plunged straight into the thick of things.

"Mr. Lomas has told me why Dr. Essenheim came here," he said. "It was to see him!"

Chapter Five

PASSED IN THE DARKNESS

THIS brief and precise announcement produced a spell of silence, during which we all inspected each other anew. Lomas looked as if he expected to be questioned; Calvert evidently wanted Heddleston to do the questioning. And presently Heddleston very quietly addressed himself to his task.

"Yes?" he said. "So Dr. Essenheim came down to see Mr. Lomas? We've rather gathered that from information given us, and we're glad to hear that Mr. Lomas confirms it."

"Who gave you any information to that effect?" asked Lomas sharply.

"Mr. Kershaw, of the Harp and Crown at Rievesley," replied Heddleston. "Dr. Essenheim asked him the way by the moorland path to Harlesden Hall."

"That all he asked him?" enquired Lomas, with what I considered a slight element of suspicion. "He's a chatterer, you know, is Kershaw – plenty of tongue, what?"

"That was all that he asked him – according to Mr. Kershaw," replied Heddleston. "A mere enquiry! But Dr. Essenheim did come, didn't he?"

"Oh! He came, right enough, did Essenheim!" assented Lomas, slapping the arms of his elbow chair and smiling as a self-satisfied man smiles who knows that he is in possession of facts not known to his audience. "Yes, he came! I reckon I'm the last man that saw him alive, poor fellow! Except, of course, the man who did it – whoever he may be. You've no idea of that, of course, Calvert?"

"None!" replied Calvert. "So far!"

"Well, there it is!" said Lomas. "He came to see me that night, as I say."

"We should be very much obliged to you if you'd tell us why Dr. Essenheim came to see you, Mr. Lomas," remarked Heddleston. "We want to clear up the mystery of his death – his murder, to be plain. Anything you can tell us – "

"Oh, I can tell a good deal!" interrupted Lomas. For some reason, unknown to us, of course, he appeared to be very well satisfied with himself, and from time to time treated us to a smile of conscious superiority. "I can tell! That's what I hurried back from town for. Of course, it's a longish story. You see, you gentlemen don't know me, nor my place – I live at Harlesden Hall."

"We have had some information," said Heddleston quietly. "And we have seen Harlesden Hall."

"Well, of course, it's a very old place," resumed Lomas. "Ours is a very old family – there was a time when we owned nearly all the land round these parts, and it isn't my fault that I don't own it now, worse luck! Of course, being an old house, there's a lot of old stuff in it – hang me if I don't have a regular systematic look through it some day and see what there is that's really valuable. However, that's neither here nor there for present purposes. What led up to this affair was this: I was turning out the contents of an old chest one day, a while ago, perhaps a couple of months ago, and I came across an old book – you'd never guess what it was!"

"No? What was it?" asked Heddleston, affecting innocence. "Something valuable?"

"It was a copy of *The Pilgrim's Progress*, written by John Bunyan – what they call the real genuine first edition, and no mistake about it!" replied Lomas, triumphantly. "Of course, I didn't know that, at the time – not me! I know nothing about books – never read 'em! But I had a notion – you see, I do read the newspapers, and I've read of the big prices sometimes given for these curiosities – I had a notion, I say, that this particular one might be worth a bit. So I put it in my pocket, and next time I was in York I showed it to Mr. Whiteley."

"Who is Mr. Whiteley?" asked Heddleston.

"Mr. Whiteley's what they call an antiquarian bookseller," replied Lomas. "A chap that knows all there is to know about that sort of thing – it's his trade, d'ye see? Well, as soon as ever he'd clapped eyes on it and turned it over a bit, he gave me a look. 'You've made a fine find here, Squire!' he says. ` Do you know what this is? 'I know what it says it is on the title-page,' says I. 'It's *The Pilgrim's Progress*.' 'Aye!' he says. 'It is that, but it's the very first edition! Not a doubt of it – I know!' 'Is it worth anything?' I asks. He gave me a fine old stare through his spectacles when I said that. 'Worth anything?' he says, scornful like, 'I should think it is worth – something!' 'What would you give for it?' says I. So he took off his spectacles then, and put down the book. 'Look here, Squire,' he says. 'It's a good job you came to me with this – some men would have done you over it. Now listen,' he says. 'There's only one man in the world who can give you the price you ought to have for this book, and that's the famous Dr. Essenheim, of New York. I'll give you his address and you must write to him, telling him what you have to offer, and asking him, next time he's in England to come and see the book. I'll do more for you – I'll draft you a letter for him – come back here after you've had your lunch and it shall be ready for you, and you can copy it when you get home.' Well, of course, I thanked him, and did as he suggested, and that night I sent the letter off to New York."

"But not the book?" asked Heddleston.

"No fear!" laughed Lomas. "No, sir – I have a safe, leastways, a strong room, at my place, and I locked up old Pilgrim in that as soon as I got home from York that day. Well, in about three weeks I got a reply from this Dr. Essenheim. He said he was greatly interested and when he came to England in October he would write to me for an appointment. And on Monday morning, October 21st, I got a letter from him which I have in my pocket-book now – here it is, and you can read it for yourselves."

He drew out of an ancient pocket-book, tied up with a bit of whip-cord, a much creased and crumpled sheet of letter paper and we all bent over it as it lay on Calvert's desk.

THE MORETUS CLUB,
985 ST. JAMES'S STREET, S.W.I.,
October 19th.
DEAR MR. LOMAS,
– I am now in England and have some business in your district on Tuesday next, the 22nd inst. Will you kindly wire to me at the above address early on Monday morning saying if it will be convenient to you to have me call at Harlesden Hall on Tuesday evening?
Yours sincerely,
CHARLES ESSENHEIM.

Heddleston handed the letter back with a question.

"You sent an affirmative telegram, of course?"

"Wired to him first thing – as soon as I'd got this letter," replied Lomas. "Yes, sir! – only too anxious to see him, of course. You see, Whiteley had given me to understand that this Dr. Essenheim would give me the biggest price I could get anywhere. 'Of course,' said Whiteley, 'I could have the old thing put up to auction – but if I did Essenheim would be sure to get it.' In Whiteley's opinion it was far more to my advantage to deal with him privately. And Whiteley gave me a good tip – not to bargain! Essenheim, he said, could give the very tip-top price. So, you see, I was all ready for him when he came."

"And – he came?" said Heddleston quietly.

"He came – right enough! Came about half-past six on the Tuesday evening. I let him in myself – my man, Chaffin, all the servant I keep nowadays, though I can remember when we'd a dozen, men and women, in the house – was out. A very nice quiet gentleman, Dr. Essenheim – Yankee, of course. I gave him a drop of whisky; he gave me a cigar, and I fetched him the book. He wasn't five minutes looking at it, then he put it on the table beside his glass and offered me five thousand pounds for it. Just that!"

"Did you accept his offer?" asked Heddleston.

Lomas made a grimace.

"Will a duck swim!" he exclaimed. "I should think I did! Wouldn't you? Five thousand pounds for a bit of an old book? Rather! And in another minute or two I'd the five thousand pounds in my pocket – cash sir!"

"Cash – eh?" said Heddleston. "Not a cheque?"

"Notes! – he'd brought 'em with him. He counted 'em out – fifty notes of a hundred each," replied Lomas. "I gave him a receipt, and there was an end of the matter. He put the old book in his pocket, and the thing was done."

"Did he leave then?"

43

"Not for a bit. He asked me if I'd any other old stuff of that sort. I showed him round a bit – there was nothing he wanted."

"What time did he leave?"

"It would be about a quarter-past seven. He told me he was going to stay at the Muzzled Ox at Kirkenmore that night and return to London by the first train in the morning. Possibly, he said, he might break his journey at York to look in on Mr. Whiteley for an hour – he knew him by name."

"Did he say anything to you of where he'd been during the day?"

"Not a syllable!"

"Didn't say anything about having bought anything else that day?"

"Not a word!"

"Well, did he know his way from your house to Kirkenmore?"

"I went down to my front gates with him and put him on the path. I told him to be careful when he crossed the top of Harlesden Scar, but assured him there was no danger there as long as he kept to the path, and that wasn't a difficult thing to do, because it's a good wide path, and he'd always feel it beneath his feet, even in the darkness."

"And that was the last you saw of him – at your gates?"

"That was the last! – of course."

"When did you first hear of Dr. Essenheim's death, Mr. Lomas?"

"Not till this very morning! I saw it in the paper when I was getting my breakfast."

"In London?"

"To be sure – at my hotel. I wired straight off to Calvert."

"You'd been to London in the interval, eh?"

"Went to London the very day after Dr. Essenheim had been to see me – set off first thing next morning. I'd important business there. As soon as ever I'd had my breakfast that morning – Wednesday – I set off. Called at the Bank in Rievesley, paid in those notes I've told you about, caught the train to York and went on to town. Of course, I was nicely upset when I read the papers this morning! And I understand that so far Calvert has heard nothing that's at all helpful. That so, Calvert?"

"We have no clue as yet," replied Calvert.

Lomas looked round the circle of faces. I could see that he had something to say, and wanted to be impressive.

"Well, I can tell you something!" he said, impressively. "There may be something in it, and there may be nothing in it. I couldn't have told you anything when I got out of the train two hours since, at Rievesley, but I can now. I called in at home on my way here, and my man, Chaffin, told me something – just something! Mind you, it mayn't be of the least importance – still there it is!"

"Let us have it, Mr. Lomas," suggested Heddleston. "Any scrap of information is valuable."

"It's more than a scrap – if there is anything in it," replied Lomas, confidently. "You see, as I told you before, Chaffin was out that night, the night, or rather evening, when Dr. Essenheim came to my place. Chaffin had come in here, to Kirkenmore, to do our week's shopping. Well, now, when I looked in this afternoon, Chaffin, of course, asked me if I'd heard of the murder. Of course, I said I had – what about it? He then said that when he was coming home that night from Kirkenmore, by way of Harlesden Scar, he met, just after he'd passed the brow of the Scar itself, a man who was walking slowly in the direction of the Scar. It was dark enough by that time, and Chaffin couldn't see the man's face. Chaffin bade him good night, but he got no reply. Chaffin went on in the direction of Harlesden Hall, and a bit further across the moor he met another man who was walking very fast and passed him at some yards' distance between them. Of course, he couldn't see his face either. That's Chaffin's story – and all there is in it. Now, I don't know what you think, but I think that first man was Dr. Essenheim and the second was some chap who was after him – the chap who murdered and robbed him. But as to who he was – well, that's your job, Calvert."

"What time did your man Chaffin get in that evening?" asked Heddleston.

"I can't say, sir – I didn't see him or hear him come in."

"He didn't mention this to you that night – or next morning?"

"He did not! There's nothing unusual in meeting a man or two on that path, you know. There's a good deal of use made of it – it cuts off a lot of corners between moorland places and Kirkenmore."

"I suppose you didn't notice anybody hanging about when you went out with Dr. Essenheim to your front gates, did you, Mr. Lomas?" enquired Calvert.

"I did not, Calvert. But Lord bless you! – it was dark then, and there might have been a dozen men hanging about. Plenty of cover round my place, as you know. Anyway, that's what I think – Dr. Essenheim was followed! The man probably watched him into my house, watched him out of it, was watching when I took him down to the gates, and set off after him when I'd gone into the house again. That, most likely, was why he was walking fast when he passed Chaffin – to catch Essenheim up. Anyhow, Chaffin, though he's a queer sort, is a dependable one, and if he says there were two men on the moor at that time, there were! And one of 'em must have been Essenheim! As for the other – well, I say it's Calvert's job to look for him!"

With that Lomas got up, and after remarking that he'd be present at the inquest next morning, went off, evidently well satisfied with himself. As for the rest of us, we dispersed, wondering.

Chapter Six

THE INDIAN ARROW-HEAD

THERE was, of course, a great deal to wonder about. If Chaffin's story was true, and if the first man he met on his homeward walk that night was Dr. Essenheim making his way to Kirkenmore past Harlesden Scar, and if the second man was some miscreant who was tracking Dr. Essenheim down to murder and rob him, the problem immediately arose – who was that second man, and where did he go after the commission of his crime? Calvert had made the most exhaustive enquiries throughout the immediate neighbourhood as to the presence of strangers in the district at the time in question, and had not heard of any whose doings could not be satisfactorily traced and explained. And yet, calmly considered, there seemed to be no reason why Chaffin's story should be taken as being otherwise than true. It formed part of the evidence put forward at the inquest next day, and though he was closely questioned by the Coroner and by a local solicitor whom Frank had engaged to watch the proceedings, he stuck to his tale and nothing shook it.

In a certain way it was the most important evidence given; for the rest, a recapitulation of the facts already known to us, through the two landlords and Lomas, pointed to no more than that Dr. Essenheim had come to the district for two specific purposes: the first, to meet the unknown lady at Rievesley; the second, to call on Lomas at Harlesden Hall; and that after making his call on Lomas he had gone away into the night to be murdered and robbed in a lonely place. But – by whom?

By this time the Yorkshire Moorland Murder, as the newspapers called it, had excited widespread interest, and at the inquest at Kirkenmore the Press was represented not only by local reporters but by representatives of the big London and provincial papers and the chief Press agencies. To these gentlemen, keen enough for news, the Coroner, before finally winding up a long day's proceedings by adjourning the enquiry for a fortnight, made a special appeal. He asked them to use their influence in the way of getting two persons to come forward – one, the young lady who had lunched with Dr. Essenheim at the Harp and Crown; the other, the man who had looked in at the Harp and Crown twice on the same day that Dr. Essenheim was there. It might be, he said, that neither could throw any light whatever on the mystery of Dr. Essenheim's murder; but, whether they could or not, it was highly desirable that they should make themselves known. Let the gentlemen of the Press do their best to induce them to come forward – however little they might be able to tell.

The gentlemen of the Press departed to write up the case in their best manner, according to the standards of their respective journals, and the little town settled into quietude for the rest of the day, though its various inns and places of resort were, to be sure, full enough of gossip, speculation, and theory as long as the bars and bar-parlours kept open. Next morning we buried Dr. Essenheim as quietly as possible in the churchyard of Kirkenmore: he had made strict provisions in his will, a copy of which Heddleston procured from his office in London, that he should be interred at the place wherein he died, wherever it might chance to be. That sad duty performed, Heddleston, Frank, and I prepared to set off to London next morning: our next job, Heddleston said, was to examine Dr. Essenheim's papers at the Carlton Hotel and at the Moretus Club, in hope of finding something – memorandum, note – anything that might give us a clue to the identity of the murderer. But on the very morning of the funeral Calvert came to us carrying a small paper parcel, the wrappings of which he proceeded to undo at the corner of our dining-table.

"I've got something here which was picked up on Harlesden Moor this afternoon by a man who was coming along by the path between Lomas' place and the Scar," he said. "It's an object that doesn't seem to belong to these parts, and I've been wondering if it was the property of the dead gentleman – dropped by him, you know. I've never seen anything like it before."

He unrolled the last wrapping of tissue-paper and laid on the table before us a curious object which, at first, to my unlearned eyes, looked like a piece of blueish-grey stone, three cornered, tapering from a wider base to a narrower point, and having, beneath the base, a sort of shaft-like termination, around which was a band of gold engraved with some inscription. At sight of it Frank Essenheim leaped to his feet, snatching at it from across the table.

"My uncle's mascot!" he exclaimed. "An Indian arrow-head from which he never parted! He always carried it in his pocket – he'd a fancy that it brought him luck. It's been in our family for generations – look at the inscription!"

We read, in turn, what was engraved round the plain gold band:

Yellow Stone River, June 5th, 1805. John Essenheim. Thou did'st preserve me in the midst of mine enemies.

"There's a family legend – or, rather, history – about this thing," continued Frank. "An ancestor of ours, John Essenheim, a hunter and trapper, escaped from a gang of Blackfoot Indians at some place on the Yellow Stone River, on the date given here, with this arrow-head sticking in him – the shaft had broken off. When it was cut out and he was recovered from the wound he put the thing in his pocket and had this gold band with its inscription fitted round the base, and ever afterwards he carried it about him. On his death, my grandfather got it; when he died my uncle Charles, the eldest son, took it over. He'd an almost superstitious feeling about it – wouldn't be parted from it! He always carried it in an inner pocket – it was a regular mascot to him! Well – it didn't avail him in the end, anyway. And this was found – where?"

"It was found, sir, on the edge of a small pond that lies on the side of the moorland path between Harlesden Scar and Harlesden Hall," replied Calvert. "It was lying in the mud at the edge of the pond, as if it had been dropped there – "

"Thrown there!" exclaimed Heddleston. "How far is this pond from the path?"

"Five or six yards," said Calvert. "It's just a bit of a pond – standing water."

"If it's five or six yards from the path," remarked Heddleston, "It's not likely that Dr. Essenheim would go to it – why should he? The path's well defined there, isn't it? Very well – why should he go off it? And as to his dropping this thing there – no! – we've just heard that he always carried it in an inside pocket. This, Calvert," he continued, picking up the arrow-head, "has been thrown aside by the man who robbed Dr. Essenheim's dead body of all there was in the clothing! And the discovery of it on the edge of that pond proves something definitely – in my opinion, at any rate!"

"What may that be, sir?" asked Calvert.

"Why, that the murderer, after throwing his victim over the edge of the rocks at Harlesden Scar went back by the way he had come!" asserted Heddleston. "In other words he went back towards Rievesley instead of going forward to Kirkenmore. He must have followed Dr. Essenheim from Rievesley, and to Rievesley back he went when he'd done what we know he did. That man, Calvert, must have been in Rievesley that night, and it's an extraordinary thing that you can get no news of him!"

Calvert threw up his hands in a gesture of despair.

"Our people at Rievesley, sir, have made every enquiry they could," he answered. "They've interviewed and questioned and cross-questioned the railway people to such an extent that we now know practically everything about everybody who came to Rievesley and went from Rievesley on that Monday and Tuesday. We know all about the strange young lady for instance – what time she arrived and was met by Dr. Essenheim, and what time she left and was seen off by him. But of that tall man who looked in at the Harp and Crown twice during the Monday – once just after lunch, and again later on, we can hear nothing. I'm sure he wasn't a railway passenger."

"There are other means of transit than those approved by railways!" said Heddleston, cynically. "There are motor cars and bicycles, and a man's own legs. Anyway, that man has got to be found, whoever he is, and whatever his business in these parts was!"

There was no more that we could do, for the moment, at Kirkenmore, and next day we returned to town and began a systematic examination of Dr. Essenheim's effects, belongings, and papers with a view to discovering something that would throw light on the mystery of his murder. There was a good deal to do at our rooms at the Carlton; he also had a private locker at the Moretus Club in which he kept some papers and memoranda; all these things had to be carefully gone through. But at the end of an exhaustive search at the hotel we had discovered nothing tending to throw any light on the visit to Kirkenmore and Rievesley, nor any reference whatever to the mysterious young lady met at the Harp and Crown. At the Club, however, we did find something. This was the letter written by Lomas to Dr. Essenheim at New York, of which Lomas had told us when he hastened down from London to Kirkenmore. It was pretty much what he had described it to be – an account, copied, of course, from Whiteley's draft, of the first edition of *The Pilgrim's Progress* which Lomas had discovered in his house, and a suggestion that Dr. Essenheim should make an appointment to see it when he next came to England. This was all we found at either the Carlton Hotel or the Moretus Club, and, while it substantiated Lomas' account of Dr. Essenheim's visit to him, it was of no help in elucidating the mystery of the murder.

By this time the police authorities were deep in the matter, and quite apart from our efforts were making their own investigations. They had a theory of their own – explained to Frank Essenheim and myself by an Inspector who called on us one day to talk over the problem. The main line of this was that the murder had been carefully planned and carried out. Dr. Essenheim, they pointed out, was well known in England. It was well known, too, that he had vast resources at his bank. Again it was well known that he dealt in large sums. Most important and significant fact of all, from the point of this police theory, was that it was also well known that Dr. Essenheim habitually carried large amounts of ready money on him in the shape of banknotes. In the opinion of the police, he had been shadowed on this last visit to England from the moment of his landing at Southampton to the time of his death. Probably, they said, he was seen to cash his cheque for five thousand pounds that morning of October 21st and to put the banknotes he received in his pocket; probably he was followed from the bank to the station, and thence down to Yorkshire – followed so cleverly that he had not the slightest idea that he was being followed. Their further theory was that more than one person was concerned in the case; there would, certainly, they thought, be two or perhaps three. The man of whom Kershaw had told us – the man who had been in the Harp and Crown bar-parlour when Dr. Essenheim made his enquiry about Harlesden Hall and the moorland path might be one: in all probability, he was one. When Frank Essenheim and I pointed out that the most exhaustive enquiries on the part of Calvert and the local police had failed to reveal the presence of a stranger – other than that particular man – in the neighbourhood of Rievesley or Kirkenmore on the two days in question, our visitor smiled, cynically – in these days of extraordinary facility in movement, he said, such adepts in crime as those he had in mind would indeed be poor hands at their craft if they couldn't avoid observation, especially amongst a set of simple rustics!

"The motive of this murder," he concluded, with emphasis, "was robbery! We are of the firm opinion that this gang – for we're convinced it wasn't the work of a single hand – knew that when Dr. Essenheim left King's Cross he'd a big amount of money in banknotes on him. Well, when it came to it, when they knocked him down at that lonely spot, Harlesden Scar, and proceeded to go through his clothing, they didn't get the £5,000 worth of banknotes. But they found on him the copy of that first edition of *The*

Pilgrim's Progress! What would they conclude – knowing his profession and all about him as they did? Why, that he'd paid away the banknotes, the whole lot, for that copy! And as he wasn't a philanthropist but a remarkably astute dealer in rare books, they'd know that the book in their hands was worth a great deal more, probably at least two or three thousand pounds more, than the five thousand he'd given for it. So – you follow me?"

"Not quite," said Frank.

"What I mean is that the gang will have to be traced through that book," said our visitor. "It'll come into view again!"

"You think that?"

"Think it? Good Lord. I'd bet on it – it's a certainty! Of course it'll come up again. We've been having expert advice on this point. There are not many copies of that first edition known. Six or seven, perhaps. This of Lomas' is outside that number. The people who've now got it will exercise the most extraordinary care about bringing it in the light again: they may, and probably will wait some considerable time, perhaps years, before they do so. But it'll reappear!"

"What method do you suppose they'll adopt?" asked Frank.

The Inspector laughed knowingly.

"Oh, they'll be up to all the tricks of the trade!" he answered. "Trust 'em for that! There'll be a careful planting of the thing. Then there'll be a Discovery – you know: a discovery in big letters. Rare find! First edition of a world classic unearthed in an unlikely place. Back-of-beyond cottage, likely, or amongst a pile of rubbish, or a barrow in Farringdon Road. Paragraphs about it in the papers – and all that. Perhaps it won't be unearthed in this country at all, but across the water, in yours, Mr. Essenheim. And perhaps neither here nor there, but in Australia. When brought into the light of day once more, it'll either be snapped up immediately by one of your millionaire collectors or be put up at auction. But – it will reappear, sure as fate!"

"Well," said Frank, quietly, "and when it does reappear how are you going to identify it with the Lomas copy? Eh?"

"Um!" replied our visitor, thoughtfully. "That, of course, is a stiff problem! But it can be done. There'll be a lot of tracing back. Anyhow, gentlemen, that's our theory, and we pin our hopes as regards a definite discovery on that book turning up again. In the meantime... well – "

He spread his hands expressively and went off. And he had not been gone many minutes when a page-boy appeared and informed us that there were two young men downstairs who were desirous of seeing Mr. Frank Essenheim on a matter of importance.

Chapter Seven

WHAT THE WAITERS SAW

I MAKE no claim to the possession of any particular power of observation and none to what I may call the detective faculty, but having some knowledge of hotel and restaurant life I had no doubt whatever as to the calling of the two young men who were presently shown in to our presence. Each wore a heavy overcoat coming down, in each case, to a little below the knee; one overcoat was of a grey mixture, the other of a brown. But below the skirts of each appeared black trousers of that sort of cloth usually associated with dress suits. From that small fact I set our two visitors down as waiters – probably on their way to their work or having got an hour off in which to make this call.

They were intelligent, sharp-eyed fellows, both, not English, though they proved to be thoroughly well acquainted with the English language, and their inspection of Frank and myself as we stood watching their entry was keen enough: plainly, they had something to tell and wanted to know who they were dealing with; perhaps they wanted to know, also, if the telling was going to benefit themselves. One of them carried under his arm a small parcel done up in brown paper: I had an idea that he regarded whatever was in it as being of value.

"You have something to say to us?" I asked as they stood hesitating. "What is it?"

The elder, a dark-eyed, olive-skinned youth, looked from one to the other of us.

"Mr. Frank Essenheim?" he questioned.

"This gentleman is Mr. Frank Essenheim," he replied. "I am Captain Mannering."

He nodded as if he knew all about me, and setting down his parcel on a side-table close to where he stood, began to search an inner pocket. From its depths he produced a handful of newspaper cuttings and, singling one out, held it towards us. On it was a portrait of Dr. Essenheim.

"We think – me and my friend here – that we can tell something about this gentleman," he said. "It's the picture, this, isn't it, of the gentleman who was found dead – murdered, they say – away in the country – Yorkshire. We've seen several pictures of him in the papers. I have them here. Cut out – with all there's been in the papers about him. We've read everything we could get hold of – interested, do you see?"

"Who are you?" I asked.

"We're both waiters at the Waldorf Hotel," he answered. "My name's Haecky – his name's Schmidt. He's in the lounge at the Waldorf; I'm in the restaurant. Been there some time – they'll speak for us there if you want to know anything about us."

"What is it that you know?" asked Frank.

"That's the point!"

"What we know is that we've seen this gentleman," replied Haecky, pointing to the portrait. "We saw him a few days before the date they give in these newspaper reports as being that of his murder. We can't be quite certain as to the very exact date when we saw him, but it was during the week previous to the 21st October."

"Where?" I asked.

"At the Waldorf. Schmidt, he saw him in the lounge; I saw him later in the restaurant. Then Schmidt saw him in the lounge again."

We had all been standing so far: now I pointed our visitors to chairs.

"Sit down," I said. "Now – you say this was during the week previous to the 21st October? You can't remember the exact day?"

"No! But it must have been the Tuesday or the Wednesday. Fore part of the week, anyway, I think it was the Wednesday."

"Had you ever seen the gentleman there before?"

"No. Not me, anyhow. Nor Schmidt, neither."

"Why did you pay any particular attention to him, then – a chance customer?"

The two men exchanged glances.

"There were circumstances," replied Haecky. "We never had any doubt, as soon as we began to see pictures of him in the papers."

"What were the circumstances?"

"One was a lady – a young lady – that met him there. Schmidt can tell that more than I can."

We turned to Schmidt. Schmidt nodded, with complacent assurance.

"It is I who see him first," he said. "Haecky – he see him later. Then – when we see these pictures of him, afterwards, in one paper and another, we say to each other, 'That is the gentleman who was here with the so-pretty young lady one day not so long ago!' Oh yes – we know him quite well, from his pictures!"

"Tell about his coming then," ordered Frank.

Schmidt settled himself, evidently not indisposed to play the part of narrator.

"It is as Haecky says," he began. "I am in the lounge at the Waldorf. Well, I am in the lounge about a quarter to one clock on the day we aren't quite certain about. Tuesday it may be, or Wednesday, of that week, middle of October. This gentleman comes in – I don't think he'd ever been in before, not in my time; also, he looked about him as if he wasn't what you call familiar with the place. Well, he sits down where he can see the entrance. Sits down and just – watches. Didn't order anything, you understand? Just sits quietly, looking where you come in. And then, after a piece, the young lady comes."

"What sort of young lady?" asked Frank.

"Well, she was a very pretty young lady. English girl."

"What was she like? Tall – dark – light – what else?"

"Oh, well, she was very pretty! Nice figure – tallish – fair hair – young. Perhaps twenty years old she might be."

"Well, she came in? What then?"

"The gentleman he went to meet her. But I shink they hadn't ever met before, you understand. My impression that was. Seemed to be asking if she was – you know? But then very friendly – shake hands and so on."

"Didn't you catch anything that was said? No names?"

"No names, no. Not at any time. Heard a bit of talk afterwards – word here and there, you understand. Nothing to speak of. About books, it seemed to be."

"Well, what happened when they met?"

"Went and sat down, side by side, and talked. Didn't order nothing – no drinks. And after a bit they get up and go into the restaurant. There, for a time, I didn't see them no more. Haecky, he sees them in there; he tells that part of it."

We turned our attention to Haecky, who appeared equally ready to discharge the narrator's task.

"Yes, I attended to them," he said. "The gentleman was very particular about the lunch, and about the wine, and he was very polite and attentive to the young lady. She was very pretty."

He nodded solemnly, as if the prettiness of the unknown had struck him more than anything.

"Everybody looked much at her," he went on. "Much admired, you understand? I think the gentleman liked her to be admired. He was, of course, much older. Nice-looking man, too."

"Did they sit long over their lunch?" asked Frank, getting to more practical matters.

"Three quarters of an hour, perhaps," replied Haecky. "Took their time, yes."

"Did you overhear anything they said – did you catch any names?"

"No names, no. And nothing much, anyway. Just talk – as people do talk over their meals. Nothing to remember."

Frank was beginning to show signs of impatience. Nothing definite was coming of this, so far. He glanced furtively at me, shaking his head. But I felt there was still more to be heard.

"Well – what happened after they'd lunched?" I asked.

"They went back to the lounge – for coffee," replied Haecky. "I didn't see them any more. Schmidt saw the rest."

"They came back to a nice corner in the lounge and I brought coffee to them," said Schmidt. "The gentleman smoked a cigar, and he and the young lady talked. He seemed to talk very nice to her."

"How long did that go on?" growled Frank.

"Oh, they sit there perhaps half an hour. Then she rise, and he walks with her out to the entrance. The man who stands there – hall-porter, you know, he tells me afterwards that the gentleman puts her in a taxi-cab and she goes away. But he walks away. And then, perhaps ten minutes after they are gone, I find the book!"

"The book? What book?" demanded Frank.

"The book what she left," replied Schmidt. "When she come in, she has a book under her arm. She took it into the restaurant with her when they go to lunch; she brings it back with her when they come for their coffee, and when she goes away she leaves it behind her. Then I find it."

Haecky reached for the brown paper parcel and began to unfold it.

"This is it," he said. "Schmidt, when he found it, he took it, of course, to the office until the young lady came to ask for it. But she has never been to ask for it, so when we decided to come here and say what we knew, we got leave to bring it with us. This is it – with a bit of card in it."

Frank snatched at the book excitedly. I knew what he was thinking – there might be a name, perhaps even a name and address in it. I felt some excitement myself as, leaning over his shoulder, I watched him turn the flyleaves.

However, there was nothing. The book itself was a copy of a novel which was just then being widely read. Had it been a copy from a library we might have traced its borrower, but it was a brand-new copy, presumably bought at a book stall or bookseller's shop, and there was not as much as an initial pencilled inside its cover.

But there was the bit of card of which Haecky spoke – the fragment of a postcard, torn off to act as a bookmark. It fell to the floor when Frank opened the book, and I uttered an exclamation as I picked it up. For there, on the correspondence side of it I saw and recognised Dr. Essenheim's writing.

There was very little of it, however. It was only a bit of the postcard that the owner of the book had made use of – scrap torn off. And all that appeared on it was this:

.....*rf Hotel*
......*about 12.45 noon.*

I turned the bit of card over eagerly, hoping to find a name and address on it. But here again was disappointment. All that remained was the postmark in the corner, showing that the card had been posted in the West End of London on October 14th, and just a termination or two below:

.....*am,*
.....*el,*
.....*outh.*

"Damn!" muttered Frank. "Worse than nothing!"

"Scarcely!" said I. "I think we might make a little – something at any rate – out of this. To begin with, what's left on one side shows that this was an intimation to the recipient that she could meet Dr. Essenheim at the Waldorf Hotel on some stated day at 12.45 noon. That's obvious! – it only needs the missing words supplying. And there's more encouragement on the other side. The letters 'am' are, plainly, the termination of the young lady's name; 'el' is the end of 'Hotel'; 'outh' the termination of the name of some place. But – what place? There are no end of places terminating in ' outh'. Bournemouth – Weymouth – Tynemouth – lots more! Still – "

"Are we going to go searching all those places for an hotel in which a young lady is staying whose surname terminates in the letters ' am'?" asked Frank. "Pretty big job!"

"I've heard of much stiffer ones," said I. "But these two men – we had better find out if they're expecting largess for their trouble in coming here. They will be, of course."

"Pay 'em and get rid of 'em," muttered Frank. "I don't see that we're much further for all that!"

"You expect some reward for your news?" I said, turning to Haecky. "Well – what do you say?"

Haecky produced a slip of newspaper from his bundle of cuttings. I knew what it was as soon as he showed it. We had empowered the various press men to announce that Mr. Frank Essenheim would suitably reward anybody who could give information about his late uncle's doings just previous to his death.

"We read this," remarked Haecky. "What we would like is that you shouldn't give us anything at all now. If what we have told you turns out to be valuable information, then we should like our remuneration to be of a corresponding nature. I understand – from this morning's paper – that you haven't had much help up to now? So perhaps we're first in the field. We'd rather leave matters till you see of what use our information is."

They went away, and Frank, hands in pockets, began to walk up and down the room.

"You're figuring that this girl of the Waldorf is the girl of the inn at Rievesley?" he said after a while.

"I am!" I replied. "Of course she is!"

"Well, in that case she's got to be found," he said. "But what licks me is – why doesn't she come forward?"

"Because she doesn't want to come forward," I answered. "If she had wanted to, she'd have come forward long since – after all this publicity. She has reasons, but – "

Here the door opened and the page-boy brought in a letter addressed to me and marked *Urgent*. On opening it and glancing at the signature I saw that it was from Superintendent Calvert, at Kirkenmore, enclosing two telegrams.

Chapter Eight

THE TWO TELEGRAMS

I READ Calvert's covering letter before opening the telegrams.

Dear Sir,

In accordance with my promise to keep you and Mr. Frank Essenheim acquainted with any new development here, I beg to say that this afternoon Mr. Whittaker, of the Muzzled Ox, came across to tell me that his wife was having the room occupied by Dr. Essenheim on the night he stayed there done out and cleaned; this had not been done since Dr. Essenheim was there, as I had given instructions that the room was not to be interfered with, pending investigations. One of the women engaged in this work found in a waste-paper basket two telegrams which had evidently been thrown away by Dr. Essenheim; you will see – as I think it well to enclose them for your inspection – that they are addressed to him at a London club. One of them is merely a message from Mr. Lomas of Harlesden Hall, and confirms what he told us. The other appears to be from the lady who on Tuesday, October 22nd, met

Dr. Essenheim at Rievesley; you will observe that this telegram is unsigned by its sender. If we could obtain the signature at the back of the original form it seems to me that through this telegram the lady could be traced.

Up to now I have not succeeded in obtaining any further local information beyond what you are already aware of.

Yours faithfully,
WILLIAM CALVERT.

While Frank was reading this I unfolded the telegrams. They had been straightened out by somebody since their recovery from the waste-paper basket, but seemed to have been crumpled up into a twisted mass before Dr. Essenheim threw them away. They were, however, quite legible. The first was from Lomas, and was addressed to Dr. Essenheim at the Moretus Club.

Thanks for letter Tuesday evening here will be quite convenient Lomas.

This had been sent off from Rievesley post office very early on Monday morning, October 21st. As Calvert said in his letter, it confirmed Lomas' story as to his appointment with Dr. Essenheim. All this was plain sailing – it neither added to nor took from our knowledge. But the second telegram was exasperating:

Will meet you Rievesley Station about 11.30 Tuesday and bring book.

No signature, as Calvert had pointed out. The mysterious lady, young, pretty, still remained mysterious – more so than ever.

"All the same," remarked Frank, after a moment's thought, "we know now why she met him at Rievesley. It was to show him a book. I figure things in this way. This is the girl who met him at the Waldorf some days previous to the 21st October. She told him at that interview of some book she wanted to sell. Probably that book was in the North of England. He knew he was going down that way; within the next few days he let her know he was going to be in the neighbourhood of Rievesley on October 22nd: her telegram – this is to tell him she'll meet him and bring the book with her. Very well – they met at Rievesley. He saw the book; he bought it – didn't that landlord fellow tell us he saw my uncle hand her a cheque? That's the cheque for £2,000 which was cashed by a lady at Bickfords a day or two later. And still – who is she?"

"This wire," I remarked, picking up the crumpled telegram, "was sent off from York. Therefore, the lady, whoever she is, was in York very early in the morning of Monday, October 21st. She sent off this wire very early – Dr. Essenheim had both these wires handed to him when he went to the Moretus Club at a quarter to eleven, and presumably they'd been there a bit before that. Well, now, as Calvert says in his letter, if she stuck her name at the back of the telegram form, and we can find it, we've a clue to her identity!"

"Are senders bound to stick their names at the back?" asked Frank.

"I'm not sure about being bound, but they're expected to, and it's the usual thing," I replied. "There's a proper space provided. The original form will, of course, be at York."

"Very well, then I guess we'll go down to York and look for it," he said. "That girl knows something and she's got to be found. I'm all the more confident she knows something because of her keeping in the dark. Why hasn't she responded to the demand for her in all the newspapers? She's got some reason for keeping hidden, and we're going to unearth her. Get a timetable and let's be off."

It was useless to suggest further consideration and delay to a young man whose pockets were full of money and his heart hot with anger against his uncle's murderers, and within an hour we were once more at King's Cross and in an express for York. We got there early in the evening and Frank insisted on beginning our investigations at once. Fortunately we had little to do; the telegram had been sent off from the railway station, and without much trouble we were permitted to see the original. At the sight of it each felt inclined to swear. For – as regards the name it was utterly impossible to make it out! There was one initial and a name following it, but whether the initial was O or Q or A we could not decide. As to the name, it appeared to begin what I took to be U; Frank thought it was V; the clerk who produced the form inclined to the opinion that it was meant for H.

"Purposely illegible!" growled Frank. He turned the form over. "Look there!" he said, indignantly pointing to the text of the message. "She could write clearly enough when she liked! And then again," he continued, turning the form back, and indicating the address given, "that's plain enough, too – Station Hotel, York. She meant her signature to be unreadable."

"For that matter," observed the clerk, with a grin, "she could have given a false name and address. We shouldn't have been any the wiser. But why not try the hotel people and see if they know anything about her? What's the date concerned? – October 21st? She may be in their register for that date."

It was good advice, and we followed it – by going into the hotel and booking rooms for the night. When we had washed away the dust of our journey there was still half an hour before dinner; we spent it in examining the register. Now, the Royal Station Hotel at York is a big one, and York is half way between London and Edinburgh, and there are a great many people who break a journey at York, to say nothing of tourists and travellers on business, so that the register is always full and has a great number of signatures in it. And although we went through it with scrupulous exactitude we could not find anything to show us that the young lady we wanted stayed there on any date between October 14th and October 22nd. We turned away from the register feeling our task to be a peculiarly exasperating one: there was nothing for us now, it seemed, but to dine, sleep and go back to London, defeated. But I had a sudden inspiration.

"While we are here in York," I said, "we ought to see Whiteley, the man to whom Lomas showed his *Pilgrim's Progress* and who advised him to offer it to Dr. Essenheim. We may be able to get some ideas from him."

"Good notion!" agreed Frank. "How do we get him?"

I glanced at the clock. It was barely seven: Whiteley would probably be at his shop yet; we might get at him on the telephone. Within five minutes I had got his address and number and was speaking to him. I told him who we were – the late Dr. Essenheim's nephew and secretary – and why we were down there, and asked him if he could come and dine with us at half past seven. He accepted the invitation with alacrity, and came along at once.

Personally, I was glad to see Whiteley. He was a middle-aged man, sharp, alert; there was nothing of the dry-as-dust, snuffy antiquary about him which I had expected. He had a good appetite for food and a nice taste in wine, and, like a sensible man, he refused to talk business over his dinner. But when we had dined, and had got into a nice comfortable corner, with cigars and coffee and liqueurs, he turned on us with a knowing eye.

"Well, gentlemen," he said, "I guess I know why you wanted my company tonight! Still investigating, eh? A stiff job! How far have you got?"

At Frank's suggestion, I gave Whiteley a full account of our doings up to that moment. He listened carefully, but I could see that he was not as much concerned about the young lady part of the business as we had been.

"Speaking for myself, gentlemen," he said, "I should put all that down to mere coincidence. I don't think that episode has anything to do with the murder of Dr. Essenheim – who, undoubtedly, was murdered, poor fellow! I think it was just coincidence that Dr. Essenheim had some transaction with the young woman you know of on the same day that he had his transaction with Lomas. The meeting with her is altogether a separate thing from what followed."

"Why doesn't she come forward, then?" demanded Frank.

"She may have a hundred reasons – for all we know," replied Whiteley. "Probably the real one is that she wishes – and has good reasons for wishing to keep her transaction with Dr. Essenheim a dead secret. Were it my affair, I should dismiss her from the case – "

"You're forgetting something, Mr. Whiteley!" I said, interrupting him. "Something, too, that, to my mind, is of supreme importance."

"Am I?" he replied. "What is it, then?"

"Just this! When this mysterious young lady wired to Dr. Essenheim – here's the wire – at the Moretus Club, telling him she'd meet him at Rievesley on Tuesday, October 22nd, she added that she'd bring the book! That, presumably, was the book which – I'm presuming again – she'd told him of when they had their interview at the Waldorf Hotel. Very well, we conclude, that she brought the book to him at Rievesley. We conclude too that he bought it from her. The landlord of the inn at Rievesley saw him give her a cheque – I take it that that cheque was for the purchase price of the book. I take it, too, that the book was then and there handed over to Dr. Essenheim and that he put it in his pocket and had it on him when he went, a little later, to call on Lomas at Harlesden Hall; was on him, too, when he left Harlesden

Hall. Now – where is that book? Gone – with the Lomas copy of *The Pilgrim's Progress*, which was also on him!"

He had listened carefully to that, and now he nodded gravely.

"Quite right!" he said. "I had forgotten that. Well, it only confirms a certain suspicion, a theory, that I've had all along. My belief, gentlemen, is that the murder of Dr. Essenheim was a carefully-planned, cunningly-arranged affair which had its origin – ah, perhaps across the Atlantic!"

We made no reply to that, and after nodding at me very solemnly and deliberately he went on:

"I never had the pleasure of meeting Dr. Essenheim," he said, "though I've often corresponded with him and have frequently done business with him. But I know several men, English and American, who knew him intimately. Dr. Essenheim, I'm given to understand, was singularly open in speech and manner. He talked freely to his friends and acquaintances about his doings and his dealings. Moreover, certain things about him got out. He was known to carry considerable amounts of ready-money on him – a bad habit! He was a man whom it was worth while robbing, in plain words. Now, my theory is that he was shadowed, had been shadowed, all the time since his landing at Southampton on this trip, and dogged until a favourable moment came. The murderers – for I think there was more than one hand in it – found the two books you mention on him and knew that they represented a big sum, and of course, they took them. Gentlemen – those two books will come to the surface, perhaps not just yet, perhaps not for years, but they will come! Mark my words!"

"The police authorities in London have the same theory, Mr. Whiteley," I remarked. "But if it's a sound one, how is it that the most minute enquiries, on the spot, have so far failed to reveal the presence of any strangers in the district on the night in question. Calvert, the Kirkenmore Superintendent of Police, hasn't been able to hear of anybody that he could suspect."

"I challenge that," he said. "I've read every newspaper account of this affair that I could get hold of, and if Calvert says there was nobody about of whom suspicion could be held, he's wrong! Who was the man who came into the inn at Rievesley when Dr. Essenheim was there? Who was the man that Lomas' man-of-all-work, Chaffin, passed on the moor as he returned from Kirkenmore to Harlesden Hall? Why has the first-named man never turned up to say who he is and what he was doing at Rievesley on that particular afternoon? Both those points require clearing up. And you forget another thing – the character of the neighbourhood in which this crime was committed: I mean the physical character. In a wild, sparsely populated district like that, men could be concealed, men could get away unobserved without the least difficulty. No, gentlemen, Dr. Essenheim was tracked, watched – his murderers were lying in wait for him when he came out of Lomas' house that night!"

We had nothing to say to that, and for a moment or two we all sat silent.

"I suppose Lomas told me all he knew?" I said at last. "I've often wondered if he did!"

Whiteley shrugged his shoulders.

"Lomas!" he exclaimed. "Oh, don't fret yourself! Lomas is a true country bumpkin – he couldn't keep anything to himself if he were offered a pension for life! I should think you could see what Lomas is – a bumptious simpleton, only too ready to blurt out every-thing he knows to anybody. Lomas – pooh!"

He took his leave soon after that, and for some time Frank and I sat in front of a bright fire in the hotel lounge, smoking in silence. I was wondering what we were going to do next, when Frank suddenly threw away his cigar and spoke:

"Mannering!" he said, "while we're in the neighbourhood we'll go to Kirkenmore again. Find out what time the first train starts in the morning."

I went across the lounge to the hall-porter. He had a railway guide in his hand at the moment I approached him and was pointing out something in its pages to a tall, dark man whom I had noticed booking a room at the office just before Whiteley left us. The man asked a question or two and turned away and I made my enquiry. The hall porter smiled.

"You're the second gentleman to ask that within five minutes, sir," he said. "That gentleman wanted an early train to Kirkenmore. Very infrequent service there, sir; it's only a branch line. The first train in the morning, sir, is ten twenty-five, arriving eleven-thirty. No change, sir."

I glanced at the other enquirer as I went back to Frank, and set him down as a superior sort of commercial traveller. He was on the platform next morning when we went to the train; he got into a first class compartment near our own. And when we reached Kirkenmore he preceded us out of the station and, after asking a question of a porter at the exit, marched straight up the one main street – to turn in at the very place we, too, were making for – the police office.

He had disappeared when we went inside; we had to wait a minute or two before gaining access to Calvert. Presently, however, we were in his room. There, seated by his desk, was our fellow-traveller, who inspected both of us with considerable interest and curiosity. As for Calvert, he wore an air of surprise and anticipation.

"Didn't expect to see you gentlemen," he explained. "But you've come in the very nick of time, as we say in Yorkshire. This gentleman – "

He waved a hand at the tall man, and the tall man smiled and spoke:

"I'm the man who called on Mr. Lomas at Harlesden Hall on the evening of Tuesday, October 22nd," he said. "And I've come here to tell all about it!"

Chapter Nine

THE OTHER MAN

THERE was something in the stranger's half-quizzical, half-amused smile which showed me at once that, whatever he might have to tell about his visit to Harlesden Hall on the evening of Dr. Essenheim's murder, he was not likely to know anything about the murder itself. He nodded at me as Calvert mentioned our names, still smiling.

"I saw you two gentlemen in the hotel in York last night, and I saw you again this morning on the train," he remarked. "If I'd known who you were, I should probably have told you what I shall now tell the Superintendent here – in your presence, I suppose. But I haven't introduced myself to you yet, Superintendent – by name anyway. Allow me – my card. Robert Filliter, gentlemen, of Warde, Filliter and Brebenham, estate agents, of Down Street – I think our name's pretty well known," he added with a complacent smile. "Old established and eminently respectable – as they say."

"What have you to tell us, Mr. Filliter?" asked Calvert, laying the card aside on his desk. "We shall be glad to hear it, whatever it is. You say it was you who called on Mr. Lomas that night on which Dr. Essenheim met his death? Well, we've been making enquiry for you ever since."

"So I understand, but I have been abroad since the 24-th," replied Filliter. "I've only just returned from Normandy – had to go over to a little place near Rouen in connection with some property for which we are agents. I didn't see the newspaper requests for my presence and evidence until yesterday noon, when one of my partners drew my attention to them. We decided that I had better run down and see you personally, at once, so I caught an afternoon train to York, where I arrived too late to catch the last train here. However, here I am, and I propose to tell you all I know. But first let me know exactly with whom I am dealing. One of these gentlemen, I understand, is the late Dr. Essenheim's nephew, Mr. Frank Essenheim? Which? Very good! Then the other is Captain Mannering, Dr. Essenheim's secretary? All right, now we know where we are: I have read of both you gentlemen in the papers which my partner had saved for me. I read them in the train, coming down. Now, gentlemen, and you, Superintendent, you will please understand that I am going to speak to you in strict confidence – the strictest confidence? If my information leads to anything resulting in – criminal proceedings, I suppose against somebody – I shall, of course, consider it my duty to give it again in the witness box. But for the present – you understand?"

We gave our assurances that we should regard Filliter's communication as strictly confidential, and he settled himself in his chair by Calvert's desk and proceeded with his story.

"Well, gentlemen," he said, "what I have to say is just this: I came down from London very early on the morning of October 22nd – Tuesday – on purpose to see Mr. Lomas of Harlesden Hall: to be precise, I came down by the 5 o'clock train from King's Cross. My object was this: You, Superintendent, are aware, though these gentlemen may not be, that the Lomas family, of Harlesden, at one time owned nearly all the land round here. Bit by bit they lost it – horse-racing, gambling, the bottle! You know what I mean. Eventually, all that remained to this present Lomas, who is, I understand, the very last of his race, and is an unmarried man, is the Hall itself and about a thousand acres of the moorland behind it. Now two or three years ago, Lomas put this property on our books for absolute disposal. From time to time we sent clients to inspect it, but we never had any offer from any of them. However, a day or two before I came down to see Lomas, we got an unexpected offer from a client whose name I am not at liberty to mention at present. He had been to see the place and its surroundings, with the result that he called on us and made a cash offer of a certain sum for the lot. So my object in coming down here on October 22nd was to see Lomas personally and put the offer before him."

"What was the sum offered?" asked Frank.

"Ah, that I am also not at liberty to say!" replied Filter. "If it should ever become necessary to say it, I shall have to say it; but at present I can't. It was a fair sum for a place that had been greatly neglected – I may say this: it ran into the thousands – not many thousands, but still thousands; and – well, nearer ten then five, and it was to be cash down and a speedy transaction. Well, as I have said, I came down on that morning. I don't know this district: I had never been north of York before. I got off the train at Wilmoor Junction, about noon, and after making some enquiries, I chartered a car from the neighbouring hotel, after getting an early lunch there. I set off in this car for Harlesden Hall – a long drive. When we got to Rievesley the driver wanted something, and went to a garage to get it. I turned into the Harp and Crown while he was thus occupied. I looked into the lounge and saw a gentleman there with a young lady – he, I suppose, was Dr. Essenheim, and the young lady was the one who, like myself, has been pressed to come forward. After remaining in the

Harp and Crown, which I'd entered as much out of curiosity as anything, a few minutes, I went away and rejoined the car. We went on to Harlesden Hall – "

"What time would that be, Mr. Filliter?" asked Calvert, who was making rough notes.

"I can't say exactly, but early in the afternoon: it was well before two o'clock, at any rate, that I called at Harlesden Hall. But Lomas was not in. At first I thought the place was untenanted, for there was no response to my repeated knockings. Indeed, I was about to go away when the driver of my car remarked that he saw a man doing something or other amongst some out-buildings in the rear of the house. I went round there and found a queer sort of individual, half indoor servant, half labourer, who was feeding some pigs. He was difficult to get anything out of, but eventually I succeeded in extracting the information that Mr. Lomas had gone out early that morning and that his return was absolutely uncertain. As I had journeyed so far on purpose to see Lomas, I pressed the man to tell me something more definite, and at last – mainly, I think, through the tempting properties of half a crown, on which he spat before pocketing it – I got out of him that his master might be found at the Gamecock and Sportsman, on the high road to Grisedale, or, if he was not there, at the Duke's Head, at Highallerton – places, as I soon discovered from a map which my driver produced, were not only some distance off, but miles apart!"

Calvert turned in his seat, pointing to a large map which hung on the wall over his mantelpiece.

"That's right, Mr. Filliter – as Mr. Essenheim and Captain Mannering can see for themselves if they glance at my map," he said. "There's the Gamecock and Sportsman, gentlemen, an old wayside inn, high up on the moors, miles away to the north-east. There's Highallerton, miles away to the north-west! Now I come to think of it, I have heard that Mr. Lomas spent a good deal of time at both."

"What did you do?" I asked, turning to Filliter after a glance at the map.

"Well," he replied, "there I was, and there was the car, and I hadn't come over two hundred miles to be easily put off. I told the driver to go on to the Gamecock and Sportsman, and off we went. It was a long ride over some very bad moorland roads."

"Sorry to interrupt you," I said, breaking in on him, "but perhaps the Superintendent can tell us something. How did Lomas get to these far-off places? Horseback?"

"Oh, Mr. Lomas has an old second-hand car – good enough to run about in over our rough roads," replied Calvert. "He and his old car are known far and near – picked it up, for a song, so he boasts!"

"A long ride – further than I'd bargained for," continued Filliter, "and bitterly cold it was on those moors. However, we reached the inn – a solitary place in a wild region. And there again was disappointment. Lomas had been there – been there for some time, but he'd been gone an hour. Where? Well, a man who had seen him leave in his car fancied – only fancied, mind you! – that he'd gone in the direction of Highallerton – fifteen or sixteen miles away. So I told the driver of my car – on the principle of in for a penny, in for a pound – to go to the Duke's Head at Highallerton, and off we went again. It was getting towards dusk when we reached it, and when I found that this was another blank covert, I was more than half-minded to throw up the chase and go back to Wilmoor Junction and return to York, at any rate for the night. But the landlord of the Duke's Head told me that he had heard Lomas say that he was going home, so I decided to go after him. We had to pass through Rievesley again, and there my driver wanted some petrol. While he went in to get it, I looked into the Harp and Crown again. In the bar the gentleman I had seen on my previous visit was talking to the landlord; I heard him asking for information about a short cut to Harlesden Hall. I went off to my car in a few minutes, and for the second time we drove round to Lomas'. And this time I found Lomas at home. He let me in himself."

Filliter paused, giving me a look which seemed to signify that he was now getting to the most important part of his story.

"I want you, gentlemen, in view of what occurred later, to pay particular attention to what I am going to tell you next," he said. "When Lomas opened his front door to me, there was a fairly bright light in the hall, from a big lamp that stood on a side-table, and in the hall, standing near an open door, was another man, a tall, well-built man in dark clothes, who, after a mere glance at me as I stepped in, turned into the doorway by which he was standing and vanished. I never saw him again. But I understand from the papers that Lomas says that when Dr. Essenheim came, a little later, he, Lomas, was all alone in the house? Well, he wasn't alone when I was there!"

"How long did you stay there?" asked Frank.

"Not long, Mr. Essenheim," replied Filliter. "I went straight to the point, and made Lomas the offer. Now, I may tell you that I know a good deal about Lomas' financial position, and I confidently expected him to jump at that offer. Very much to my surprise, he didn't! Indeed, he seemed as if inclined to give it a blank refusal. But all of a sudden he sort of veered round. 'I'll tell you what I will do, Filliter,' he said. 'I'll give you a definite answer within twenty-four hours – by wire. Will that do?' I said it would do – certainly. 'All right,' he said. 'You'll hear from me yes or no by six oclock tomorrow afternoon.' Then he offered me a whisky and soda – and a few minutes later I was back in the car and going for Wilmoor Junction. I got some dinner at the hotel there and returned straight to town by the night mail. And – "

"A moment," interrupted Frank. "Did you see that man again – the man you spoke of just now?"

"I didn't. He didn't come into the room in which Lomas and I had our talk, and he wasn't in the hall when I went out of that room. But I'd a very good view of him at the time of my entrance."

"Can you describe him?"

"Yes! He was a tall, well-built man, dark of hair and complexion, and I should say about thirty-five years of age. I should have set him down as a professional man. Of course, you must remember that I only saw him for, literally, a moment. On seeing me he turned into an open doorway and vanished. But he was there – which makes it strange that Lomas should say that when Dr. Essenheim called he, Lomas, was alone. For Dr. Essenheim must have called within a few minutes of my leaving, as far as I can reckon things."

"Stop a bit!" said I. "Did Lomas say he was alone? Didn't he merely say that his man Chaffin was out when Dr. Essenheim called?"

"That's more like it," agreed Calvert. "That's what he did say. Still, I thought that he meant that he was alone. However – "

"Go on about Lomas himself," interrupted Frank brusquely. "Did you hear from him next day?"

"Yes!" replied Filliter. "But not in the way he'd indicated. At three o'clock on the following afternoon – I mean the afternoon following my visit – Lomas himself walked into our office, and said that he'd come to give us his answer in person. He'd accept the offer I had made him, on a strict condition – that the transaction was to be carried through and the purchase money paid over immediately. Harlesden Hall once gone, he said, he was going to leave England for good!"

Chapter Ten

GONE!

BY this time we were all three pretty deep in thoughts and reflections of our own as to the precise value and significance of Filliter's information, and for a minute or two there was silence. Calvert, as a practical man, broke it with a direct question.

"And has that been done, Mr. Filliter?" he asked.

"The transactions completed?" said Filliter.

"Yes! As a rule these things – conveyance of property, you know – take some little time. But they can be carried out quite speedily if need arises. As Lomas was insistent on urgency, matters were put in hand immediately by the solicitors on both sides, and the affair was concluded during my absence in Normandy. Yes! – the purchase money was paid over to Lomas a few days ago, so my partner tells me."

"Who's the purchaser?" asked Calvert. "No secrecy about that, I suppose? We shall all get to know him here very soon, no doubt."

"A Mr. Marston, a retired gentleman who wanted a place on these moors with a bit of shooting, fishing and hunting attached to it," replied Filliter. "Of course, he'll have to lay out a good deal on repairs at Harlesden Hall, and he'll not get into residence there just yet."

"Is Lomas still there?" he enquired.

"I don't know – I suppose he may be," answered Filliter. "He was in town last week – he called at our office one day, I'm told."

"What's he going to do about his belongings?" asked Calvert. "Furniture, and so on?"

"Can't say – I've no knowledge," replied Filliter. "Sell all there is there, I should think, if he's going to leave the country."

Calvert turned in his chair and looked at Frank and then at me.

"What do you gentlemen suggest, after hearing this story?" he asked.

"I suggest precisely what I'm going to do," replied Frank. "I'm going out to find Lomas! I want to know who that fellow was who was in the house when Mr. Filliter called there. I want to know, too, why he never mentioned his presence."

"Well, I've been considering what I remember about that matter," remarked Calvert. "Captain Mannering there is right! Lomas never did say that he was alone in the house when Dr. Essenheim called. What he did say was that he let Dr. Essenheim in himself because his man Chaffin was out, away here in Kirkenmore, buying things. If Lomas had a man there, I suppose he saw no call to mention it."

"He gave the impression, in his talk with us here on his return from London, that he was alone," persisted Frank. "His evidence at the inquest gave the same impression. There was all along the idea that he and Dr. Essenheim were in the house alone; that he was alone when Dr. Essenheim left him."

"He may have been," said Calvert. "The man Mr. Filliter saw in the hall may have left soon after Mr. Filliter left, and before Dr. Essenheim arrived."

"I'm going to know who that man is!" said Frank, doggedly. "Because I believe he's the man that Chaffin saw on the moor. Come on, now – let's get some car and get out to this place."

"My car's outside," said Calvert. He looked enquiringly at Filliter. "Are you disposed to go with us, Mr. Filliter?" he asked. "Or are you wanting to get back?"

"I'll go with you," answered Filliter. "I'm as curious as you are. And if we find Lomas there I've no objection to your telling him that I saw a man in his hall, whose identity you want to establish. Between ourselves," he continued as we all rose, "it seems to me a very queer thing indeed that Lomas should have had a man there that evening of whom nothing has been heard in the course of your enquiries! I understand from the newspaper accounts that you've ransacked this district."

"Couldn't have done it more completely, sir, than it's been done!" declared Calvert. "Me and my men have spent the whole of our time – we've little to do here, as a rule – in prosecuting enquiries. And who this man that you saw can have been, and how he got there, and how he got away from there, beats me hollow!"

We went out to Calvert's car and he drove us across the moors to Harlesden Hall. I had expected to find it closed and lifeless, but as soon as we reached the entrance gates we saw that there was a good deal going on there. Three or four large furniture vans stood in the neglected and forlorn pleasure grounds in front of the house, and into these workmen were conveying the old furniture from within. Evidently Lomas was losing no time in making a thorough clearance.

"Those are Watkinson's vans," remarked Calvert as we walked up the grass-grown drive. "Watkinson of Highallerton, furniture dealer – I guess he's bought the entire contents of the house! There is Watkinson," he continued, as a stout, elderly man came down the steps, superintending the removal of a fine old sideboard. "He'll know where Lomas is, if he's anywhere about. 'Morning Mr. Watkinson! – pretty busy, eh?"

Watkinson removed a wide-brimmed hat and mopped his forehead with a big cotton handkerchief of strong colours. He favoured us, as a body, with a questioning, suspicious glance – I think he took Frank, Filliter and myself for detectives.

"So – so, Superintendent," he answered indifferently. "Got to get the whole place cleared out by tomorrow night. Painters and decorators coming in, d'ye see?"

"I see," assented Calvert. "Mr. Lomas about anywhere?"

"He is not, sir," replied Watkinson, again mopping his perspiring forehead. "Haven't seen Mr. Lomas since last week. Left these parts for good, I believe."

"After selling you his belongings, eh?" suggested Calvert. "Lock, stock and barrel, no doubt?"

"As you say, Superintendent, lock, stock and barrel! He got me over here, showed me what there was, asked for a cash offer, accepted it when I made it, and there you are! Now, some of this good old stuff," continued Watkinson, pointing a fat forefinger towards sundry articles – "some of it, I say – I hope to sell to this gentleman who's coming in here – it ought, of course, to be put back where it's stood for many generations. But it wants touching up a bit and repairing a bit – fine stuff when I've done with it, I assure you! No sir, I can't say where Mr. Lomas is. But between you and me and the post I've a notion."

"Let's have it!" said Calvert.

"I think he's gone abroad, Superintendent – over the seas and far away! Going to try his fortunes in another climate. Got a bit of capital to go on with now, you see, by selling house, land and belongings."

"You've settled up with him, then?"

"Settled up with him there and then, sir! Cheque down on the spot – that's my way. And a very tidy sum, too. Good old stuff, this, you know, Superintendent."

"I dare say you'll do well enough out of it," remarked Calvert, dryly. "You'd know more of its value than he would. But I say – where did you see him last?"

"Where? At my office, in Highallerton, three or four days ago. He was off then – at least, I gathered he was off to London."

"Goodbye, eh?"

"So I gathered," assented Watkinson. He replaced his hat, and from under its brim re-inspected the rest of us. "Want him – for anything?" he asked, suddenly.

"We wanted some information from him," replied Calvert. "That's all. Have you seen that man of his anywhere about – Chaffin?"

"I know Chaffin. No! – at least, not since yesterday, when we started operations. He was in charge of the house when we arrived and gave me the keys. After that he cleared out and I – I haven't seen him since."

A man in an apron, standing near, turned to us.

"Chaffin told me he was going to live in a cottage at Rievesley," he said. "Mr. Lomas did the handsome by him, Chaffin said – fixed him up comfortable."

"I know that Mr. Lomas gave Chaffin furniture for a cottage," remarked Watkinson.

"Maybe he's pensioned him off. Been a long time in the family, Chaffin had."

Calvert drew us away to his car.

"Well – what about having another go at Chaffin?" he asked. "He told his tale, though, at the inquest – I doubt if we shall get any more out of him. To be sure, he wasn't asked anything – because we didn't know anything then – about this man that Mr. Filliter saw."

"We'll see Chaffin," said Frank. He turned a resentful eye on the dismantled house as we moved away from it. "I don't like all this at all!" he growled. "There's some damned mystery centring round that place that I want to get to the bottom of! That fellow Lomas, now! – do you think he's really gone right away?"

Nobody could answer that question – and nobody knew where Lomas was likely to be found in London. But Chaffin might know; Chaffin might have an address: we went off to Rievesley to find Chaffin.

"I don't expect to get anything out of him," observed Calvert to me as I sat at his side in the front of the car. "Chaffin told his tale, what there was of it, at the inquest."

"Yes, but he wasn't questioned as to whether there was anybody in the house with Lomas that evening," I replied. "That never came up."

"Never came up, of course, because we'd no idea of it," said Calvert. "But you may be sure of this, sir – if Lomas had some man there that night and as he's kept the fact dark if he had, you may be quite sure that he wouldn't let Chaffin know anything about it. Harlesden Hall is a big, roomy place – a dozen men could be stored away there without anyone knowing."

"Well, it's very evident that Lomas had somebody there," I remarked. "Mr. Filliter is positive on this point. Now do you attach any significance to the fact that Lomas never mentioned this?"

"Why, frankly, I don't!" he said. "Lomas would probably say, 'What's that got to do with the Dr. Essenheim affair?

That's one matter – my visitor is another.' That's how he'd look at it – being a North-countryman. In other words, he saw no call to volunteer the statement that he had somebody in the house. The only thing that puzzles me is that during our investigations we never heard of anybody being there, going there, leaving there! However, we shall do no harm in asking Chaffin a question or two."

We found Chaffin in the bit of garden in front of his cottage: he received us in the same surly, taciturn fashion which had always been his distinguishing characteristic whenever I had seen him. He turned to his task of digging when Calvert's car drew up at his gate, and as it was plain that nothing would induce him to come to its side, we had to leave the car and go to him – a proceeding which he regarded with manifest disfavour.

"Now, Chaffin, my lad!" said Calvert, with the easy familiarity of one countryman to another. "Getting things a bit straight, like? I hear Mr. Lomas has fitted you up for the rest of your life, what?"

Chaffin made no reply – in words. He grinned sourly and grunted, all the while watching us furtively as if wondering what we wanted with him.

"We've been looking for Mr. Lomas at the old place," continued Calvert. "We've a bit of business with him. Do you know where he is, Chaffin?"

Chaffin looked round the four corners of the universe before he replied. When words came to him they were slow and surly in tone.

"I've no idee where Mr. Lomas is," he answered. "Left these parts, he has."

"Well, didn't he say anything to you about where he was going when he left?" asked Calvert. "Must have told you something, now?"

"He didn't tell me nought! I've heard him say something about foreign parts – that's all I know. I reckon he's gone there – foreign parts."

"London, maybe, eh?" suggested Calvert.

"It may be. He said foreign parts."

"Didn't leave you any address to send letters to, eh?"

"There's been no letters, nought of that sort."

"Well, there's a question or two I wanted to ask you, Chaffin. You remember that night when you passed those two men on the moor – don't you?"

"I told all about that at the Crowner's 'quest," muttered Chaffin, "Can't recollect no more now what I told then."

"Well, you can perhaps recollect this," persisted Calvert. "When you got home to Harlesden Hall that evening, after passing the two men, had Mr. Lomas any company with him – any friend stopping in the house? Think now!"

Chaffin looked sharply from one to the other of us. I had set him down from the first as a dull-witted fellow, but I now began to wonder if he was as dull as he looked.

"Nobody as I knows of," he answered. "I never see'd nobody. There wasn't anybody there when I went out to do my bit o' shopping at Kirkenmore. Mr. Lomas his-self, he warn't in when I went out – he'd been out in his car all day. He'd come in when I got back. But he went out again in his car after that."

I saw Calvert – metaphorically – prick up his ears.

"Oh!" he said. "Mr. Lomas went out in his car again that night, did he? Where did he go and at what time was it?"

"I dunno where he went," declared Chaffin. "I heard him get the car out and set off when I was going to bed, ten o'clock that 'ud be. He hadn't come back, neither, when I got up at six o'clock next morning. Then he come in and had his breakfast and set off again – said he was going to London, that time."

Calvert suddenly brought this interview to a conclusion, by turning abruptly back towards his car. As he set foot on its step he glanced round at the three of us.

"There's something, gentlemen!" he exclaimed. "Why should Lomas go out that night? Where did he go? But I've an idea! He took away the man that Mr. Filliter saw in the hall – the man who was there in the house, somewhere, when Dr. Essenheim was there!"

Chapter Eleven

UNEARTHED!

SOME idea of that sort, I think, was in the mind of each one of us. And each, no doubt, shared in the opinion which Frank voiced.

"That reopens the whole question!" he said. "Was Lomas telling the truth when he volunteered his statement?"

"Some of the truth, sir, no doubt – and not all of it!" exclaimed Calvert. "I'm beginning to suspect that he didn't tell us everything. Yet he seemed straightforward enough, and I should never – from what I know of him – have credited him with sufficient imagination to have invented things – I always considered Lomas a fool. But fools can be crafty! And perhaps he's shown craft. We've got to remember that he was candid enough about certain matters. He came straight back from London to tell his tale: that's one fact. He told us what Chaffin had told him about passing the two men on the moor: that's another. But now there are two other undoubted facts to deal with – first, he had some mysterious man with him that evening; second, he was out in his car most of the night. All that wants clearing up. And the next thing is – where is Lomas?"

"Vanished!" remarked Filliter laconically. "And – with plenty of money in his pocket!"

We went back to Kirkenmore. As the car drew up at the police-station Whittaker, the landlord of the Muzzled Ox, came across the little square from his front door, waving a telegram.

"Wire for you, Captain," he said, handing it to me. "Came an hour ago. I saw you and Mr. Essenheim setting off with Mr. Calvert this morning, so I judged you'd be coming back here."

I tore open the envelope. The message was from Heddleston, to whom we had telephoned our movements just before leaving the Carlton.

Come back at once important news for you.

That was all. And all we could do was to snatch a hasty lunch at the Muzzled Ox and set off for York and London by the next available train. Filliter returned with us. We parted from him at King's Cross with the understanding that he was to help us in tracing Lomas – but as his firm had finished its transactions with Lomas there was little prospect of his assistance doing any good.

It was too late then to go to Heddleston's office, but we knew his private address, and we drove off to that. Before giving us his news Heddleston wanted to know ours: when we had told him all we had discoursed or heard at Kirkenmore he shook his head.

"Lomas will have to be found!" he said. "There is something he has kept back. But what, now, is the important, the most important point, of the whole thing? Just this: when the murderer, or murderers, took Lomas' copy of *The Pilgrim's Progress* from Dr. Essenheim's dead body they also took the book which, without doubt, Dr. Essenheim had purchased from the mysterious young lady who lunched with him at Rievesley."

"Well?" asked Frank.

"Well – we've found the young lady!" said Heddleston.

Neither of us spoke for a moment – I think we felt that at last we were going to see daylight. Then I said what, I suppose, we were both thinking:

"She's come forward, then?"

"No replied Heddleston. "She's not only come forward, but she doesn't even know that we've unearthed her! And after all, the process of discovering her identity hasn't been so very difficult. You know that Dr. Essenheim handed her a cheque at the inn at Rievesley? Well, a few days after that – on some day during the week of his disappearance – a cheque for two thousand pounds, made payable to bearer, was cashed at Bickford's bank by a lady, who was undoubtedly the young lady of whom we have heard so much. She took the money in Bank of England notes, the numbers of which were of course noted by the bank. Well, I got Bickford's to make special and private enquiries about those notes, and this morning we got the results of those enquiries. The twenty one-hundred pound-notes paid out to the young lady at Bickford's were paid in, en bloc, next day by a young lady to her private account at a bank at Bournemouth, and her name and present address were given by that bank – under pressure, of course, and in view of the seriousness of the case – to Bickford's, and through them to me. So now – we know who she is! But, I repeat, she knows – nothing; nothing, I mean, of our enquiries or our knowledge. And from what her bankers told Bickford's, it's a damned queer business!"

"Who is she?" asked Frank, abruptly.

"The young lady is a Miss Audrey Varnam, the only daughter of a Colonel Varnam," replied Heddleston. "Colonel Varnam, when he's at home, lives in Bootham, York – he's a retired Army officer, pretty old, I believe. I say when he's at home, for he appears to have been more or less of an

invalid for some time, and is obliged to spend his winters in
the South of England. And since the beginning of October he
and his daughter have been at the Coast and Channel Hotel
at Bournemouth – where the young lady is to be found. Now
bear in mind that this is all private information given in strict
confidence, by word of mouth, by one banker to another,
and only given because, first, this affair of Dr. Essenheim's
is, without doubt, a case of deliberate murder and robbery,
and second, because Miss Varnam's evidence, whatever it
may be, is absolutely necessary. As I said in beginning, she
knows nothing whatever of the fact that her identity has
been established."

"What do you propose to do?" I asked.

"I propose," replied Heddleston, "that we all three go
down to Bournemouth tomorrow morning. We will see the
bank manager there who is concerned in the matter and
get him to arrange an interview. That, of course, must be
arranged! Whatever the young lady's feelings are as regards
her wish to be kept in the background, she will have to put
them clear aside. But with a pledge of secrecy on our part
I've no doubt she'll be comfortable – anyhow, whether she
likes it or not, now that we know who she is, she's just got to
speak."

"Do you know if she's aware of the enquiries made for her
in the papers?" asked Frank.

"I don't. But she can't have failed to notice them,"
replied Heddleston, "which makes the whole thing still more
mysterious. She's evidently some very strong reason for not
wishing to come into the limelight – what it can be I can't
imagine. Well, we've got her, and we've got to use her! Meet
me at Waterloo tomorrow morning."

We were all three in Bournemouth by one o'clock next
day, and at Heddleston's suggestion left our baggage at the
station and went off to inspect the Coast and Channel Hotel:

his notion was that we might put up there and get a glimpse of Miss Audrey Varnam before securing an interview with her through the bank manager. The hotel proved to be a quietly-situated residential house, in the best part of the town, and after booking rooms and sending for our things from the station we went into its coffee-room for lunch. And there, all unknown to her, we made our first inspection of the young lady about whom there had been so much speculation and mystery. For while we were lunching there came into the room, alone, a girl who, still alone, ate her lunch at a small table not far from ours and whom we felt certain to be the pretty young lady described in more or less detail by the Rievesley landlord and the Waldorf waiters. Anything less like a figure in a murder mystery could not have been found! She was just a slim, pretty English girl, probably two- or three-and-twenty years of age, winsome, charming, who looked as if she had nothing to conceal and no particular cares to worry her.

But that Miss Audrey Varnam had cares and responsibilities on her hands we were very soon to ascertain. As the three of us sat in the lounge of the hotel after lunch, smoking and considering our next plans, there emerged from a ground-floor corridor a small procession in which Miss Varnam figured. It was headed by Miss Varnam herself, controlling a couple of dogs, held in leash; then came a middle-aged nurse, in uniform, and finally, in a big bath-chair, wheeled by its attendant, an old gentleman whose face was the colour of mahogany, made all the darker in hue by his almost white moustache and mutton-chop whiskers, and who, in spite of his apparent infirmity of limb, had all the fierce aspect of the old, die-hard warrior. He stared hard at everybody in the lounge as his little cortege passed through, nodded grimly to one or two people whom it pleased him to recognise, and was duly conveyed outside into the sunlight of the gardens and the promenade.

"Indian Army, I'll bet!" whispered Heddleston? "Curries- – chutney – brandy pawnee – liver – gout! Poor girl! Well, I'll go and call on this bank manager: you fellows can go for a walk and see the town."

He went off, and Frank and I presently went out on the sea-front. We turned after the little procession in which Colonel Varnam was the leading figure. Without seeming to do so, we saw a good deal of its doings, and we came to the conclusion that what, with her dogs and her father and his nurse and his bath-chair, Miss Audrey Varnam had plenty of occupation.

Heddleston met us later on.

"I've fixed things!" he said. "It so happens that Miss Varnam has to see the manager on business of her own at ten-thirty tomorrow morning, and he'll break this affair to her and pave the way to our interview with her. We're to go there at eleven. And bear in mind that she's to know nothing except that we have ascertained her identity – never mind how – and have approached her bank manager as intermediary, and that everything she says – or can be induced to say – is to be regarded as of a strictly confidential nature. So, in the meantime, you young men are to keep your eyes off her!"

That was somewhat difficult. Miss Varnam dined alone again that evening: her father evidently never showed in public. And it was somewhat difficult for two young men to avoid glancing now and then at an undeniably pretty girl; occasionally, too, I caught Miss Varnam looking at me, and now and then at Frank, and sometimes at Heddleston. And there was a little amused smile of recognition about her lips when we entered the bank manager's private room next morning to be duly introduced to her. And however

THE YORKSHIRE MOORLAND MYSTERY

reticent she had been about coming forward, it seemed to me that now that she had been discovered she was much more composed and far cooler about the whole business than we were – two of us, at any rate.

The bank manager, as intermediary, put us all at our ease very quickly. He'd explained to Miss Varnam, he said, exactly who we were, what we were after, and how absolutely necessary it was that she should tell us all she knew. Miss Varnam, he went on, understood matters, and was willing to tell – all she insisted upon was that her story was to be regarded as being told to our ears alone. If it became necessary to make it public – well, that would require further thought. But she had no objection now to telling us all she could tell about her transactions with Dr. Essenheim. And therewith he invited Miss Varnam to tell her story.

"But where do you want me to begin?" she asked, glancing from one to the other of us. "You see, I met Dr. Essenheim twice."

"Begin at the very beginning, my dear young lady!" said Heddleston. "Go back to the very origin of – everything. How did you come into contact with Dr. Essenheim? Begin with that!"

"Well, it was this way," began Miss Varnam: "I think you saw me with my father yesterday afternoon? My father is a retired Army officer – Indian Army – and for some years his health has been very poor, and it is absolutely necessary for him to spend the autumn, winter, and spring months in the South of England. When we are really at home we live in York, but York is impossible for him except in summer. Of course it costs a great deal, living in hotels, and he is obliged to have a nurse, too. And some little time ago – I found that well that matters were beginning to be rather straightened in the way of money – you understand?"

"Perfectly – perfectly!" agreed Mr. Heddleston.

"And really, I had to begin to think what was best to be done," continued Miss Varnam. "My father leaves all financial matters to me, and of late – during the last year or two – he never seems to understand that money does not last for ever. I absolutely had to do something, and I thought of a plan by which I could raise a considerable sum of money – at least, I thought I could. I procured something which I believed to be of really great value – a book!"

"A book!" said Heddleston soothingly. "Just so – a book! And – what book, may I enquire?"

"A *Book of Hours*, of the 15th Century," replied Miss Varnam. "My grandfather – on my mother's side – was a famous book-collector well-known in the North of England. When he died his library was sold, but he left me the most valuable thing he had, this *Book of Hours*. It was kept – I kept it – securely locked up in our house at York; now and then I showed it to people. It is a most beautiful book – but you are waiting to know about Dr. Essenheim. Well it occurred to me that I should sell this book. The only thing was that I dare not let my father know of such a transaction! He would have been furious! His idea was that it should be passed on in our family from generation to generation. However, I determined to sell the book if I could, and in such a fashion that my father would never know that it had been sold – after all I was selling it for his sake and comfort – "

"Most admirable – exemplary!" murmured Heddleston admiringly.

"The next thing was – to whom could I sell it?" continued Miss Varnam. "Well, I made quiet enquiries, and I heard of Dr. Essenheim. I wrote to him at his New York address. And early in October I got a note from him, asking me to meet and lunch with him at the Waldorf Hotel in London. So – we met."

Chapter Twelve

WHO WAS THE SECOND?

"YOU took the *Book of Hours* with you, of course?" suggested Heddleston.

"No," replied Miss Varnam. "That was in York – locked up in a safe place at our house there. We were here at Bournemouth when I first wrote to Dr. Essenheim. I went up to town specially to meet him at the Waldorf. All I could do that day was to tell him about the book, its history and so on, and explain my position with regard to it. He was very kind about it, and he made a suggestion, which was that if he decided to buy the book he should pay me there and then a certain sum on account of the sale and should hold the book until after my father's death, so that my father should never know that it had been sold. That being settled, the next thing was to show the book to him. I was going down to York for a few days just then, and Dr. Essenheim said that he, too, was likely to be in that neighbourhood about the same time and would write to my York address. He did so, suggesting Tuesday, October 22nd, at Rievesley, and on Monday, October

21st, I wired to him from York saying that I would meet him at Rievesley next morning. We met there as arranged and had lunch together at the hotel. And then we came to terms about the sale of the book."

"May we know about that?" asked Heddleston. "This is all in strict confidence."

"Yes, I have no objection to telling you," replied Miss Varnam. Dr. Essenheim, after examining it, told me that my *Book of Hours* was very valuable – he said that he had no doubt whatever that it was worth £7,000 or £8,000. He could get some such price as that for it in America, he said, without doubt. Of course, I was delighted to hear this, but it was necessary that my father should not hear of my transaction. So Dr. Essenheim made a proposal. I was to let him have the book for ultimate sale. He was to give me £2,000 on account, there and then. He was to deposit the book with his bankers in London, and they were to be instructed that if it was ever necessary for me to produce it to my father I was to be allowed to take it for that purpose. On my father's death, Dr. Essenheim was to sell it outright for me – he said he knew of at least two famous collectors in America who would give the price he had mentioned for it – and he was to hand over the balance due to me less fifteen percent commission. I accepted this offer and he gave me a cheque for £2,000 and put the book in his pocket."

"I believe you cashed the cheque yourself at Dr. Essenheim's bank in London a few days later?" asked Heddleston.

"Yes – as I passed through London on my return here," replied Miss Varnam. "I had purposely asked Dr. Essenheim for a bearer cheque because I didn't want anybody to know about the transaction. I drew the money in notes and paid them in to my account here as soon as I reached Bournemouth. And that," she added, looking from one to the other of of us, "that is really all I can tell! Dr. Essenheim saw me off at the station when I left Rievesley for York, and of course I never saw him again. I was very, very much concerned when I heard of his death. And I have wondered ever since what has become of my book. You see, I can't do anything about that lest my father should hear of what I did. He would be terribly angry – and he would not understand."

"It is a difficult and a very delicate position," said Heddleston. "But we must hope to find a solution. Well, now, Miss Varnam, there is more that you can tell us. You found Dr. Essenheim a pleasant companion – good company, eh?"

"Oh, very – a most delightful companion! His talk about books was most charming – I was really sorry to leave him!"

"He told you a lot, I suppose, about his doings, his adventures in the book-collecting way?"

"Oh, yes – it was positively exciting – like a fairy tale, some of it!"

"Dr. Essenheim had the reputation of being a very friendly, candid man," observed Heddleston, "and of talking very freely and openly to his friends and acquaintances about his transactions – he was, in fact, the sort of man who opens his heart and mind to anyone he was well-disposed to. So now I am going to ask you a very, very important question! Much depends on your answer to it. Now listen! Did Dr. Essenheim, while you were with him at Rievesley, tell you why he was there? There – at that particular place? Think!"

But Miss Varnam's ready reply showed us that there was no need for thought or reflection on her part. She answered at once.

"Oh, yes! He told me that he had come there to see two men who had for sale what they believed to be a first edition of *The Pilgrim's Progress*."

This artless reply produced an effect on three of her listeners which Miss Varnam must have considered surprising. Heddleston, about to let out some exclamation, suddenly checked himself and turned in his chair to stare at me and Frank. But Frank was watching Miss Varnam, and nothing but a sudden tightening of his lips showed his appreciation of the real meaning of her answer; as for me, I daresay I sat open-mouthed, wondering.

Heddleston slowly turned from us to Miss Varnam, who by this time was realizing that what she had said was producing some extraordinary effect.

"Did – did I understand you to say two men?" he asked softly. "Two?"

"I said – two!" replied Miss Varnam. "Two men!"

"Did Dr. Essenheim say who they were?"

"No, he didn't."

"Or where they lived?"

"No!"

"What did he say?"

"Only that he had come down from town specially to see what had been reported to him as a genuine, undoubted first edition of *The Pilgrim's Progress*, the property of two men in that neighbourhood. He didn't mention their names, nor where they lived – but I think he did say that he was going to see them after he had seen me."

"Nothing else?"

"Oh, well, he talked a little about first editions of *The Pilgrim's Progress*, and how very scarce and rare they were, and how difficult it was for anybody other than a very clever expert to tell what was an undoubted first edition. Much of what he said was far too technical for me. I remember asking why an undoubted first edition of *The Pilgrim's Progress* was such a very rare thing, and he replied that it was because the book was so popular and so widely read when it first appeared that it was literally read to bits – thumbed and fingered to rags, he said. I remember too, that he said there wasn't, or hadn't been, more than half a dozen perfect copies in existence – known at any rate."

"Did he seem to think that this copy he was going to see would turn out to be another perfect one?"

"He laughed about it. He said it was quite possible that, despite the report he had received about it, it might turn out to be not a first edition. Still – it might."

"That's all you can recollect, Miss Varnam?"

"That is all I can recollect."

"Very well," said Heddleston. "Now we come to another phase of the matter. When you left Dr. Essenheim at Rievesley on the afternoon of Tuesday, October 22nd, he had on him – in his pocket, you said, I think – the *Book of Hours* which you have been telling us about? Well, we know that he purchased the first edition of *The Pilgrim's Progress* of which he told you. So it comes to this – when Dr. Essenheim was murdered that night he had in his pockets your book, which he valued at £7,000 or £8,000, and another book for which we know he had just paid £5,000 in cash. Now, whoever murdered Dr. Essenheim robbed his dead body, and there is little doubt that the murderer's real object was those two books! So – they are in the murderer's possession. But – you don't want publicity?"

"No – no, I don't!" said Miss Varnam. "If matters can be arranged so that my name doesn't transpire – "

"We will do our best," agreed Heddleston. "Be reassured for the present."

Presently Miss Varnam left us, the bank manager attending her to the door. When they had left the room Heddleston turned on us.

"Two men!" he exclaimed. "Two – he had to see two! Who was the second?"

"We've known there were two for the last forty-eight hours," growled Frank.

"Yes – but we didn't know that Dr. Essenheim was expecting to deal with two!" said Heddleston. "All we knew was that he expected to deal with one – Lomas! Now we hear of two who had an interest in the sale. Who was the other? Who was the man who was with Lomas at Harlesden Hall that evening and whom Lomas undoubtedly got away in the dead of night? Who?"

I put in there a remark which I had been wanting to make for some time.

"Why did Lomas come back specially from town and tell what seemed to be a plain, unvarnished tale to Calvert and to us?" I asked. "He need not have said a word!"

Heddleston laughed scornfully.

"I can answer that question, Mannering, in one word," he said. "Bluff!"

"You're suspecting Lomas – at last?" I questioned.

"I'm beginning to," he answered. "Not perhaps, of murder, but of some complicity, or knowledge, or something. Well, there's one thing certain. This thing has now got to a stage – with us – at which we shall have to hand over all our acquired knowledge elsewhere. We must now tell all we know to Scotland Yard."

"Scotland Yard is already at work," said I.

"Through Calvert," he replied. "Yes – but neither Scotland Yard nor Calvert knows what we know. The authorities at Scotland Yard must be put in possession of every scrap of our knowledge immediately. For – we want Lomas!"

We thanked the bank manager for his services, went back to the hotel, packed our bags, and prepared to leave for town. But Frank contrived to get a few minutes' interview with Miss Audrey Varnam before leaving. It was in a corner of the lounge, and out of the way of inquisitive eyes; but, without being a Paul Pry, I saw him give her something, and I happened to know what that something was – a small book which had been one of the late Dr. Essenheim's most cherished personal possessions and which Frank had found lying on his uncle's desk at the Carlton Hotel on his arrival and had promptly annexed. I gathered from this little incident that Miss Audrey Varnam had made an impression on Mr. Frank Essenheim and that he had decided resolutions on the subject of improving his acquaintance with her.

However, there was sterner business on hand, and business that it was necessary to transact immediately. Heddleston, unaccompanied, went off to Scotland Yard as soon as we reached town, and two hours later 'phoned us to go to his office. We found him there in company with a big, military-looking man, alert of eye, bristling of moustache, who might have been a sergeant-major in the Guards.

"Detective Inspector Kimberley," said Heddleston. "Mr. Frank Essenheim – Captain Mannering. Mr. Kimberley," he went on, "has assumed special and particular charge of this case. He is now fully acquainted with every detail known to us, and everything that came out at the inquest, and everything that's been in the newspapers. He's setting to work on the job himself, but he would first like to have a talk with us, and to hear any suggestions. As for me – I have none! I'd rather leave matters in his hands. But if you have – "

"Tell 'em what we have been talking about," said Frank, nodding at me. He was naturally reserved and in his own opinion no great hand at talking, though ready enough in action. "Put it straight!"

"Mr. Essenheim and myself have been discussing matters since we parted from you at the station two hours ago, Mr. Heddleston," I said. "We think that publicity ought to be given to the theft of the two books. We think that all booksellers, second-hand booksellers, book-collectors, auctioneers, and custodians of private libraries all over the world should be advised. Miss Varnam's name needn't come into the matter. We think all this because it seems abundantly evident that the thieves will sooner or later want to dispose of the books. They probably know the full value. We suggest that this should be done at once, through the medium of the Press."

Heddleston looked at the man from Scotland Yard.

"What do you say, Kimberley?" he asked. "Does that commend itself to you?"

Kimberley, who sat nursing a very square jaw on hands crossed over a silver-topped walking-cane, lifted his head and shook it.

"Well, no, Mr. Heddleston!" he replied. "Frankly, it doesn't. I wouldn't do that, gentlemen – just yet, anyway. Those fellows, whoever they are, or the fellow, whoever he is – for you don't know yet whether this was the work of one man or two – they, or he, have got the books, and what's more than that, they, as Captain Mannering observed, know their value. Well, they'll be in no hurry to sell – no hurry to bring them into the light of day. In my opinion when they do see daylight again it'll not be in this country – it'll be in yours, Mr. Essenheim. So – wait! Wait as regards that, at any rate."

"And – in the meantime?" growled Frank, who had chafed a little under this advocacy of what seemed to him a policy of procrastination. "What are we to do about that? Sit down and trust to luck? Because – "

"By no means, sir!" said Kimberley. "I propose to go full steam ahead in another direction. The first thing to do is, not merely to bring Lomas to light, but to ascertain all we can about Lomas' doings not merely on the evening of the murder but during the preceding twelve hours. I propose, gentlemen, to go down to the district concerned by the night train to York, and first thing tomorrow morning I shall begin to find out all I can about Lomas' movements on Tuesday, October 22nd."

Chapter Thirteen

THE OLD INN

I HAVE said that Frank Essenheim was essentially a man of action, always fretting to be doing something practical. This characteristic in him came out now. As soon as he heard Kimberley's proposal he jumped to his feet with an exclamation of glad relief.

"That's talking!" he said. "And I'll go with you, if I shan't be in the way? Anything's better than hanging about doing nothing, and wondering."

"You'll not be in my way, sir," replied the detective with a smile. "You can come with pleasure. And Captain Mannering, too, if he likes. You both know that country already, I understand – I don't – and you may be highly useful. And," he added, turning to Heddleston, "it's up there, I think, that we shall find whatever that there may be to a solution of this affair. First thing tomorrow morning, then, gentlemen."

So next morning found us bound Northward again – I had travelled over it so much during the previous two or three weeks that I was beginning to know every furlong of the two hundred miles between London and York by that railway line. And early in the afternoon we were at Kirkenmore once again and introducing Inspector Kimberley to Calvert, who gazed on his fellow policeman with interest, for Kimberley, we had learnt, was a personage of some fame in the detection of criminals.

"What do you propose to do, Inspector?" asked Calvert. "I'm afraid there's nothing new come to hand since these young gentlemen left me."

"Well, these young gentlemen have posted me up pretty well in the old stuff," replied Kimberley. "In fact, I think I may say I'm quite conversant with the entire history of the case as far as it's gone. As to what I propose – well, to begin with, I should like to go over the ground covered by Lomas on the day – Tuesday, October 22nd – on which Dr. Essenheim came to Harlesden Hall. Am I right, now, in what I've got? According to the evidence of his man, and to what Mr. Filliter told you, Lomas on that day got into his car, and leaving Harlesden Hall went first to – where's my note of it? – yes, first to the Gamecock and Sportsman, on Grisedale Moor, and then, later, from there to the Duke's Head at Highallerton, where he stayed until latish in the afternoon, returning to his house some time a little previous to Mr. Filliter's call on him. That all correct?"

"Quite correct, according to our information," agreed Calvert.

"Very well – I suggest making a round of these places, in your company," said Kimberley. "I suppose you're known to the landlords of these inns?"

"Well enough – everybody knows the Superintendent of Police!" laughed Calvert. "You want to question them?"

"Judiciously – judiciously!" replied Kimberley with something like a wink. "Not too insistently, of course. And that'll depend on – what sort of men they are."

"Oh, well, I know 'em both quite well," remarked Calvert. He reflected awhile in silence.

"We'll go in my car – now," he continued. "It's only three o'clock, and we can do a lot before evening. But – I think you'd better leave the talking, or most of it, to me, Inspector. They're both queer chaps, these two landlords – one of 'em particularly so – and you're a Londoner. Now, these folk, men of the moors and dales, are always suspicious of a Londoner, and – "

"Oh, you do the talking!" laughed Kimberley.

"I'll listen – if there's anything worth picking up, I shall get it. We'll leave it to you, Calvert – you'll know how to do it."

"Oh, I know how to do it!" assented Calvert, with a grin and a wink. "You gentlemen are three friends of mine out for a bit of a ride round the country, eh? We drop in at these places for a friendly glass and a cigar, like, and we pass the time of day with the landlord or whatever company happens to be present, and we talk a bit, and lead the talk on to the Moorland Mystery as the newspaper chaps call it, and – well, if we hear anything worth hearing I reckon we shan't have cotton-wool in our ears! That's the way of it, Inspector! Now, if you were to walk in and say 'I'm the famous Detective Inspector Kimberley, of Scotland Yard, and here's my warrant card, and now what can you tell me about this, that, and t'other?' – well, you might as well expect to get butter out of a dog's throat as get any information from a Yorkshireman. Leave it to me – and now we'll be off. My car's always ready."

It was a raw, gloomy November afternoon, that, and when we had cleared Kirkenmore and got up on the lonely moors the cold was intense and the wind, blowing across from the North Sea, twenty miles away, keen and searching. I was not sorry when, after running for some miles over a road which wound in and out over valley and hill, Calvert, by whom I sat in the front seat, pointed to a house that stood out at some distance against the skyline.

"That's our first objective, Captain," he said. "The Gamecock and Sportsman on Grisedale Moor. Used to be a famous house of call that, in the old days before the railways came this way. This road that we're on now was the only means of communication between the middle of the county and the north-east coast and the Gamecock was a sort of half-way house for the coach and the post-chaise and so on. And they do say that it was a resort of smugglers, for all that it stands so far inland – may have been, for there's cellars under it and running away from it that you could store the cargoes of half a dozen ships in. That's the sort of place it was in what folk call the good old days."

"And now?" I asked. "Come down in the world, eh?"

"Oh, now," he murmured – "now it's like a lot of them old coaching inns – a mere shadow of itself. The licence has always been kept up, and there's a fair amount of custom from the farmers and shepherds round about, and in summer a lot of pedestrians and tourists go past, and if need be they can put a traveller up very comfortably – artists sometimes stop there to paint pictures of the moors. But you can see for yourself that it's about as lonely a spot as you could find."

We were by that time close to the inn, and I saw that it was all that Calvert described it to be – a big, gaunt, grey pile standing by the side of a winding moorland road. The house itself, a four square erection with an unusually high roof, was flanked by extensive outbuildings, the coach-house and stables of a former era, but there was not a sign of life about them, and nearer acquaintance showed that they were falling into decay. The whole place indeed, suggested absolute solitude, save that outside the front door a farmer's light gig stood, its horse, covered with a rug, drooping its head as if asleep. All round lay the moors, dark, dank, their uppermost edges veiled in white, curling mist. Absolute solitude – and yet only that morning we had threaded our way through the teeming traffic of London.

Headed by Calvert and admonished by him to play our parts, we left the car and went into the house. There was a comfortable, old-fashioned bar-parlour on the right of the big stone-paved hall, and in it burned a big cheery fire. A man having the appearance of a sheep-farmer, and much wrapped up in a caped great-coat and a heavy shawl, sat near it, with a steaming glass of rum and water at his elbow: behind the bar lounged a big round-faced man, whose small eyes twinkled at the sight of Calvert and ourselves.

" 'Afternoon, Super!" he said affably, as we walked in. "Bit o' joy-riding, what? Nice day for that, what?"

"None o' your jokes, Grice!" replied Calvert. "Cold as Christmas up here! – that's what it is, my lad! Friends o' mine," he went on, waving a hand in our direction – "just running 'em round a bit, eh, to see what you're like up this way."

"Well, I said you were joy-riding, didn't I?" retorted the landlord. "And as to cold, why it's always cold up here, and sometimes it's colder than at other times. What can I do for you, Super, now – drop o' the usual, eh?"

"Four o' the usual," commanded Calvert. "Keeps very good whisky, Mr. Grice," he explained to the rest of us. "And very good cigars – which is your best box, Grice?"

"Everything's of the best in this establishment, gentlemen," said Grice, with a grin. "All of the first quality – patronised by the nobility, clergy and gentry!" He pushed a box of cigars across the counter and proceeded to pour out the whisky. "Aught new down your way, Super?" he enquired, as he placed the glasses before us.

"Don't know that there is," replied Calvert, indifferently. "Well, here's luck, gentlemen! Have one yourself, Grice.

No – naught much now, I think – naught that you're not acquainted with, anyhow."

The man sitting by the fire turned and gave Calvert a staring look.

"Haven't you got to the bottom o' that moorland murder yet?" he asked, half teasingly.

"You're a nice lot, you police, to let that there go all this time without finding who done it!"

"You'd better have a go yourself, Mr. Ramsbottom," said Calvert, good-humouredly. "You can, you know, if you like."

"I've summat a deal better to do nor that!" retorted Ramsbottom. "Finding some o' my sheep i' these here moors is more my line nor finding murderers! He'll be slipping through your hands, will that chap, Super, if you aren't a bit sharper nor you have been! Haven't you got no ideas, like?"

"We don't tell 'em, if we have," replied Calvert. "But we would like to hear yours if you have any."

Ramsbottom rubbed his chin, took a pull at his glass, and shook his head.

"It's always seemed to me that Lomas was the man to tell a bit more than what he did," he observed. "Lomas was on the spot, so to speak. But they tell me Lomas has left the neighbourhood for good. I hope he's paid up what he owed. Did he settle up with you, Grice? – I know he were i' your debt considerable."

The landlord, who was leaning over the counter, listening to the exchange of words between his two customers, wagged his head and smiled.

"Aye, he settled with me, did Lomas!" he answered. "Yes – he kept his word that time right enough. And time he did, too!"

"Why, was he owing you money?" asked Calvert.

"I should say so! You see," replied Grice, "Lomas, he was a queer 'un. Used to spend a lot o' time here – not exactly drinking, but idling his time away: of course, he'd naught to do. He'd come up here for hours at a time, and as oft as not he'd get his meals here – dinner and tea and supper. And he'd stand treat to anybody who was in – if they took his fancy. He'd do that whether he'd money on him or not, and as oft as not he had no money, ready cash. When he'd no money it made no difference – he'd spend more than usual, if anything, when he was spending on tick. And of course when he was spending on tick it was put down to him – but the queer thing was that next time he came with money on him, and sometimes a good deal, he'd never dream of paying off the old score! That ran on – and it began to come to a fair old lot, I can tell you!"

"What d'ye call a fair old lot?" demanded Ramsbottom.

"Well, it was over a hundred pounds, anyway, for drinks, and cigars, and meals, and such like," replied Grice. "A hundred and twenty odd, that's what it was!"

"But you got it?" asked Calvert.

"Oh, I got it!" said Grice. "I never doubted I should get it, some day. But I'll tell you how I got it. The very last time Lomas was in here would be about the day – I believe the very day on which, according to the papers, afterwards, he sold that old book to the American gentleman: he was here some time that day, was Lomas. And I showed him his account in my book and suggested, like, that it was about time he paid up. 'All right, Grice!' he said, pleasant enough, 'you shall have a cheque in a day or two – I shall be rolling in money after tonight,' he said. 'I'll see to it!' But he didn't say how he'd come to be rolling in money – not a word o' that. Of course, after reading his evidence at the inquest in the newspapers, I knew what he meant when he said he'd be rolling in money after that night – he knew he was going to sell that old book to the American gentleman, and he'd a pretty good idea of the price. Anyhow, I got the cheque right enough."

"When?" asked Calvert. "At once?"

"Might be a week later," replied Grice. "I was a bit surprised when I saw it – not that he'd sent it, but that it was on a London bank – "

I saw Calvert give Kimberley a slight nudge of the elbow. Whether Kimberley felt it or not, I don't know – he affected very little concern in the landlord's story and seemed to be most intent on inspecting an old oil painting which hung on the panelled wall by which he was standing.

"A London bank!" exclaimed Calvert. "Bit surprising, that, as you say, Grice."

"Aye, for he did bank at Rievesley," agreed Grice. "However, there it was – cheque on the London and Universal Bank, Aldgate Branch. Met right enough. And that's the last I've seen or heard of Lomas. They tell me he's gone abroad."

"Ever heard to what parts?" asked Calvert.

"No – heard naught! But I did once hear him say that if he ever sold Harlesden Hall and got a fair price he'd go and try sheep-farming in Australia," answered Grice. "So maybe he's gone there."

Ramsbottom groaned derisively.

"Him try sheep-farming!" he exclaimed. "Lord bless yer! – he knows naught about sheep! Sheep-farming in Australia? He'll lose what money he carried with him!"

Then the talk drifted into matters connected with sheep and presently we said good day to Grice and his customer and went out to the car. Calvert turned to Kimberley.

"Well," he asked. "Any good?"

"Excellent!" said Kimberley. "Couldn't have been better. We know now that Lomas has a banking account at the Aldgate branch of the London and Universal Bank! That's a very convenient thing to know. Show me where a man banks and I'll soon show you the man! Where next, now?"

"Across country – to Highallerton," replied Calvert. "Turn up your coat-collars!"

We set off again, westward this time, across the darkening moors. It seemed to me that the winding, zig-zag track we followed was symbolical of our quest for news.

Chapter Fourteen

BIT BY BIT

IT had grown dark by the time we reached Highallerton, after a long and dreary ride across the bleak moors and through the windswept valleys beyond them, and we were all glad to see the blazing fire that burned in the bar-parlour of the Duke's Head. This was a very different house of call to that we had left an hour before on Grisedale Moor, a somewhat pretentious hotel standing in the main street of the little town, up-to-date in its appointments and boasting a smart barmaid behind the counter to which, chilled to the bone, we instinctively turned. What Calvert expected to glean in the way of information in these surroundings I could not conceive, but that he knew well enough in what waters to cast his line was soon made evident. For as we stood round the fire warming ourselves there came into the room a bustling sort of man who, after a sharp glance at us, gave the Superintendent a smile and a nod.

"Hullo, Calvert," he exclaimed cheerily. "Not often we've the pleasure of seeing you in these quarters – except at Assizes, what? What brings you here?"

"Oh, just been having a spree round, like, with my friends," replied Calvert, indicating the rest of us. "Been over the moors during the afternoon, and jolly cold it is up there!"

"Well, here's fire and there's whisky – both good restoratives," said the man, laughing. "And if you will go on the moors at this time of the year – but I say," he went on, suddenly changing his bantering tone, and coming nearer, "as you are here, I might as well ask you a question – I've been wanting to see somebody from your quarter of the world. Do you know where Lomas has gone to?"

Calvert turned a sharply enquiring eye on his questioner.

"Why?" he asked, abruptly.

The landlord glanced at me – from me to Frank, from Frank to Kimberley. There was another question in his glance.

"All friends here!" muttered Calvert, reassuringly. "You can say what you like! They – know who Lomas is."

The landlord motioned us away from the counter, at which two or three other men were lounging, to a quiet corner, where he motioned us to sit down round a table.

"I see," he said understandingly. "Professional friends of yours, no doubt. Well, about Lomas – he's left this neighbourhood, eh?"

"So I'm told," agreed Calvert.

"For good, I hear," said the landlord.

"I've heard the same," assented Calvert.

"But you don't know where he is?"

"No more than you do! You want him?"

The landlord drew his chair nearer to us and leant across the table.

"Well, I'll tell you," he answered. "Of course, Lomas used to come here a good deal – spent a fair lot of his time here, one way or another, either in this parlour or in our billiard room – you know what he was. Well, he was in here one afternoon – it would be about a week before the news of that affair at

Harlesden Scar, with which his name was connected, came out – and I mentioned to him, friendly like, that he'd an account here which ought to be settled – I did so because he seemed to be flush of money – "

"What was the account for?" asked Calvert.

"Oh, I don't know, in particular – drinks, cigars, billiards, cash lent, meals, and so on," replied the landlord, indifferently. "He went on tick a good deal, you know, and of course I knew the money would be safe. Anyway, there was a bill owing, and I mentioned it to him – just mentioned it, you know – no pressing. And – "

"What was the amount?" interrupted Calvert.

"Sixty odd pounds – sixty-seven, six, three, to be precise. Not a vast amount, but still too much to lose, you know."

"Are you losing it?" asked Calvert, dryly.

"I'm telling you! To go on – I mentioned it to him, and he there and then wrote out a cheque for it. 'You asked at what they call the psychological moment, whatever that may be, my boy!' he said. 'There you are and my blessings with it!' So – that was that!"

"You got it then," said Calvert.

"I got the cheque! On the Rievesley Bank it was – payable to me, of course. Well, I put it away in my safe with other cheques and so on – I don't pay in to my bank every day nor yet every week; and as a matter of fact it was ten or twelve days after that before I did pay Lomas' cheque in to my account. Well – it came back!"

"Dishonoured?" exclaimed Calvert.

"Well, scarcely that, I think," replied the landlord. "It was marked 'Account closed'. I thought that a bit queer – still, I gave Lomas the credit of thinking that my cheque had been cleared before he closed his account. However, a day or two after that I had occasion to go over to Reivesley on business, and I just looked in at the bank and made an enquiry. I know the cashier there, well enough, and told him what I was after. He told me – between ourselves – that Lomas had transferred his account to a London bank – the London and Universal, Aldgate branch – and that if I sent the cheque there they'd probably meet it, on Lomas' instructions. I said that it would be far better if I sent it to Lomas himself and asked him to send me another cheque on his new bank in its place. But he didn't know Lomas' address – nothing but that he believed he'd gone to London. So then I asked him – in confidence – you know – if there'd be funds to meet it if I did send it to this London bank. He laughed at that and said he mustn't reveal secrets, but he added that he didn't think I'd any need to fear. Lomas had left these parts well equipped for the future."

"He said that, did he?" remarked Calvert. "Well, of course he'd sold his property."

"Aye, and sold it very well, I'm given to understand," said the landlord. "However, this cheque. I sent it, a day or two later, to the London and Universal, with a letter explaining the circumstances, and asking them to see Mr. Lomas about it next time he called in there. What do you think came back?"

"Can't say!" replied Calvert. "The cheque?"

"Cheque, aye, and a letter!" exclaimed the landlord. "And precious little there was in the letter, too! Just a mere line to say that Mr. Lomas had closed his account at their bank and they were unaware of his address. What d'ye think of that, Calvert? Closed his new account within a few days of opening it!"

"Transferred it elsewhere, I should think," replied Calvert, after a pause. "You should have enquired of the London Bank."

"I did! I'd another letter from them this very morning," said the landlord. "Shorter than the first! – seemed as if whoever wrote it wasn't in over a good temper! Regretted they were unable to give any information about Mr. Lomas. So – there you are!"

"There you are, you mean," replied Calvert. "Well, all I know is that it's said that Lomas has gone abroad. Perhaps he has – perhaps he's going. But look here, as you've asked me a question, I'll ask you one! Was that occasion of which you speak the very last occasion on which Lomas called here?"

"It was! Never seen him since."

"Do you remember the exact date?"

"I can give you it in one minute," replied the landlord. He pulled out a pocket-book and extracted a slip of paper. "This is the cheque I've been talking about," he continued.

"The date's on it. October 22nd."

"He was here in the afternoon, you say?" asked Calvert.

"Yes late in the afternoon."

"Well," said Calvert, "do you know where he went when he left here? Did you hear him say anything?"

"I didn't. But my man outside who looks after the garage, he might be able to tell you something; he had Lomas' car in charge. Why? Are you looking for Lomas?"

"Never mind!" replied Calvert. He signed to the rest of us to rise, and presently we followed him out to his car. "Wait here!" he said. "I'll speak to that chap in the garage alone." He went off – to return a few minutes later, nodding his head at us. "I know where Lomas went when he left here that afternoon!" he whispered, "he went to Wilmoor Junction! We'll go there too."

But when we reached Wilmoor Junction Calvert did not turn his car towards the station; instead, he drew up at the Station Hotel, opposite the arrival platform.

And into the hotel he led us – to halt all three of us in the hall.

"Look here!" he said in a whisper. "I know the landlord of this house particularly well – he's an old personal friend of mine, and there's no need of any round-about work with him. I'm going to ask him some straight and plain questions! Whatever's said to him won't go any further. So – you understand?"

We understood – and we followed Calvert into a parlour where a stout, elderly comfortable-looking man was taking his tea at the corner of another welcome fire. His broad face widened into a grin at the sight of our leader.

"Hello, my lad. Didn't expect to see you at this time o' day!" he exclaimed. "Just in time for a dish o' tea – what d'ye say, you and your friends. Say the word! The lass'll have some fresh made in two minutes."

"We shan't say No, Jim," replied Calvert. "Come in very welcome, day like this." He waited until the landlord had rung a bell and given an order to the strapping girl who answered, and then, signing to the rest of us to follow his example, drew up a chair to the fireside. "Jim!" he continued, assuming an air of confidence. "We've called to see if you can give us a bit of information – I think it's probable you can. You know Lomas of Harlesden Hall?"

The landlord nodded significantly.

"Aye, I know Lomas!" he replied laconically. "What about him?"

"You know that his name came up in connection with this Harlesden Scar affair? He was believed to be the last man to see the murdered man alive?"

"I read the papers about it. Inquest and so on. And, of course, I've heard local gossip."

"What have you heard in that way, Jim?"

"Well, of course, you know how people will talk! There's folk about who hold to the opinion that Lomas knew a deal more than he ever let out. Happen he did! A queer chap, you know, Lomas! But what're you after now?"

Calvert turned in his chair, pointing first to Kimberley and then to Frank and myself.

"Well, I'll tell you, Jim," he replied. "This gentleman here is Inspector Kimberley, of the Criminal Investigation Department at Scotland Yard; these other gentlemen are interested in this case. We've got an idea that Lomas didn't tell all he knew; that Lomas knows something which we're anxious to find out. We've been tracing his movements on the day preceding the murder. We've traced him from his house to Grice's place on Grisedale Moor – the Gamecock, you know – and then to the Duke's Head at Highallerton. He left the Duke's Head latish in the afternoon and came away towards Wilmoor Junction. Now then, I want to know if you can remember if he called in here that afternoon? The exact day and date was Tuesday, October 22nd."

The tea came in just then, and for a minute or two the landlord occupied himself in pouring it out and handing round hot and generously-buttered toast to us. When we were all provided he poured out a fresh cup for himself and sipped it reflectively.

"You'll find that good tea, gentlemen," he observed. "Best Orange Pekoe, is that tea – I got it special from a friend o' mine who's in the tea trade in London. Well, this here Lomas, Calvert – yes, he did come in here that afternoon! It would be close on five o'clock – a bit after the down express from York's due."

"You're sure of the date?"

"I can fix the date – October 22nd. We'd had an auction sale here, in our big room – some house property. Yes – that same afternoon."

"Was he alone?" asked Calvert.

"No, he wasn't. He'd a man with him. That's another thing that makes me remember it."

"Why?"

"Because I'd an idea – and I have it still – that I'd seen that man before, somewhere, though I couldn't place him. But I felt sure I knew his face. Very like I'd seen him on a racecourse. Yes, the two of 'em came in to our bar-parlour – I was there at the time. They didn't stop many minutes – they'd a couple o' whiskies-and-soda and then went off. Lomas had that old car of his outside."

"Do you know in which direction they went?"

"I do – for I watched 'em go off. Rievesley – which, of course, is the road Lomas would take if he was going homeward."

"Did you hear any particular talk between them – and was there any with you?"

"No more than a remark or two about the weather. Naught more!"

"Well, this man who was with Lomas? Can you describe him?"

"I can! For, you see, with thinking I'd seen him before, I took particular notice of him. A tall, spare dark chap, dark hair and eyes and bit of a dark moustache – one o' these here new-fashioned sort o' moustaches, in the middle of his top lip. Another thing – he'd a very old, worse-for-wear trench coat on; one that I should ha' thrown away myself. But he unbuttoned it while he was in here, and underneath he'd a very smart suit on – big check suit. That was another thing that made me think I'd met him on a racecourse. Horsey-looking sort o' chap, you know. And he'd a small suitcase with him. Altogether, I reckoned that he was somebody that Lomas had come to meet at the junction."

Chapter Fifteen

AN IMPORTANT FIND

WE presently went away from this third place of call, convinced of a fact that was rapidly assuming serious and significant proportions. There could now be no doubt whatever that on the afternoon of Tuesday, October 22nd., the all-important date in this sequence of events, Lomas met, by appointment, at Wilmoor Junction, a man whom he then took home with him to Harlesden Hall. Equally without doubt, this was the man that Filliter had seen at Harlesden Hall when he called there not long after Lomas and his companion had returned. And this man, in all probability, was still there when Dr. Essenheim paid his visit in the evening.

"And he is, of course, the second man of whom Dr. Essenheim spoke to Miss Varnam," said Calvert. "And, also of course, it was to cart him off somewhere that Lomas took his car out again that night. Where? Probably to some distance, for Chaffin said Lomas wasn't back till early in the morning of the following day. But who is he? And what do you suggest doing next, Inspector?"

Kimberley had done little more than listen all the afternoon, but I had seen that he was taking in everything he heard: I saw, too, that he was thinking a good deal.

"While I'm here I should like to see Harlesden Hall and Harlesden Scar," he replied. "I suppose you and your men have combed over both of them pretty well, but I'd like to take a look at both."

"That's easy enough," said Calvert. "Harlesden Hall's in process of being dismantled, but you can see it, and as for the Scar, there's nothing to prevent that. Tomorrow morning, then, after breakfast – you'll all be stopping the night at Kirkenmore, of course?"

That, of course, was what we did, and we spent the evening after dinner in discussing and rediscussing the new features of the case. We got Whittaker, the landlord, in, and extracted from him all he knew and could tell about Lomas – his habits, his character, the company he kept and so forth. Whittaker knew Lomas well and what he did with himself and who his intimates were – they seemed to be chiefly of the horse-racing, dog-fancying variety. But we could hear nothing of any man corresponding to the tall, spare, dark individual with a slight cast in one eye who had been described to us by Calvert's friend at Wilmoor – he remained a mystery-man, hidden in clouds.

"Never mind!" said Kimberley, as we separated at bedtime. "He exists, somewhere! Our job is to unearth him!"

We went on with our job as soon as we had breakfasted next morning, going first, in Calvert's car, to Harlesden Hall. The workmen were still busy there, and had now removed nearly all the fittings and furniture. But Kimberley, prying around, poked his head into a small room opening off the hall, and having glanced at its interior motioned the rest of us towards him.

"Room here that seems to be untouched," he said. "Just, I should say, as its late owner left it."

One of the workmen, passing by, glanced into the room and nodded his head.

"Left to the last, that, sir," he remarked. "Naught in it but rubbish – most of it's to be burned."

"Well, we'll look round before you burn it," said Kimberley. He beckoned the rest of us inside and closed the door. "Lucky we came before they started their bonfires!" he continued, with a meaningful wink. "To begin with – look there!"

He pointed to a chair, a crazy, dilapidated thing in a corner of the room, on the back of which, carelessly flung there, was an old trench-coat, stained with mud and rain, and otherwise so much worn and the worse for wear that the wonder was that anybody should recently have worn it. At sight of it, Calvert let out a sharp exclamation.

"That's similar to what my friend at Wilmoor described last night!" he said. "What the strange man was wearing over a smart suit. Like to his description as one pea is to another! Now I wonder –"

"You needn't!" interrupted Kimberley. "This is the coat your friend described! It would be a bit too much of a coincidence that there should be two trench-coats – and what's this, pray?"

He had picked up the coat and was looking it closely over, and suddenly he pointed to a dark stain on the right-hand cuff, at a spot in the surface where the stuff still retained some of its freshness. As we all gathered round to stare at it, Kimberley put the tip of his fore-finger between his lips, moistened it, and applied it to the stain. The next instant he looked round at us and shook his head.

"Blood!" he exclaimed. "Well – "

He shook his head again and began to fold up the coat in careful folds; this done, he picked up a piece of brown paper from the floor and made a neat parcel of his find, while the rest of us looked on in silence. Suddenly he laughed.

"The old game, Calvert!" he said. "These chaps, they always forget something – some small detail, however carefully they plan things. Shouldn't mind laying all I've got to nothing that this will hang that chap we've heard about – when I've laid hands on him! For you may be sure, gentlemen – sorry to refer to it, Mr. Frank – that that bloodstain came from – you understand? Well – we're having some luck now, Calvert! I can see how the coat came to be left here. The fellow threw it aside, probably with instructions to Lomas to burn it – and Lomas forgot! They always forget something – always! They tell me, some of these prison-warders who have the nasty and unpleasant job of watching over convicted murderers in their last days, that their charges spend a good deal of their time – that is when it's utterly useless to keep up a pretence of innocence – in regretting what one might call lamentable oversights. It's ' If I'd only remembered this!' or 'If I hadn't forgotten that!' all through. But there's always some little thing they forgot, or some little thing they didn't remember – same thing, isn't it? There you are! Well, let's see if there's anything else in this rag-and-bone shop!"

The place was little better than that – a veritable refuse-heap. Yet it looked as if Lomas had used it constantly and perhaps been fond of it. In the one window stood an old ricketty desk covered with newspapers, letters, documents, miscellaneous objects from tobacco-pipes to fish-hooks. There were rows of old boots; old garments of various descriptions hung from pegs in the walls or were thrown indiscriminately on decrepit chairs. In one corner rested a collection of fishing-rods; in another stood several guns, their barrels rusted red. On a shelf near the desk stood a collection of sporting books, neglected and dusty; on the ledge of the desk itself were a dozen or so numbers of *Ruff's Guide to the Turf*. And fastened to one wall was a cabinet of birds' eggs, and to another a collection of moths and butterflies, all dusty and worm-eaten. The only signs of recent occupancy were seen in a half-finished bottle of whisky, which, with a jug of water and two dirty glasses, stood on a small side-table.

Kimberley gave his attention to the papers on the desk, many of which were letters of a fairly recent date. He began to go through these methodically, laying each aside as he inspected it. Suddenly he let out an exclamation and turned on us with a smile of triumph.

"Here you are!" he said, waving a postcard at us. "Another example of how these fellows forget little things! See this? Note the message, the date, the postmark. Well, Calvert, the luck's turning our way!"

We all gathered round to look at the postcard. It was addressed to Hird Lomas, Esq., Harlesden Hall, near Rievesley. On the reverse side were two lines:

All right – will meet you Wilmoor Junction about quarter to five tomorrow afternoon.

There was no signature. But as Kimberley said, there was a date and a postmark. And the date was October 21st, and the postmark was Leeds.

Kimberley got up from the desk, put the postcard in his pocket-book, and picked up the parcel in which he had packed the trench-coat.

"The next move is to Leeds!" he remarked. "Mine, anyhow! How do I get there, Calvert? I don't know this big county of yours at all, you know."

"Rievesley to York, York direct to Leeds," replied Calvert. He looked at his watch. "You can get a train to York from either Kirkenmore or Rievesley in an hour from now. Better go back to Kirkenmore – you'll want your bag, of course. What do you suggest doing at Leeds, now?"

"I suggest trying to find the owner of this trench-coat," replied Kimberley. "That's what!"

"There are half a million people in Leeds," observed Calvert.

"Very likely! There are seven million people in London – or more – but I've ferretted out a man from amongst them on lesser chances than this affords!" replied Kimberley. "To Leeds I'm going, anyway!"

"We'll go, too!" said Frank. "Seems to me we've struck some sort of a trail, at last, and I'm going to follow it!"

We went back to the Muzzled Ox, collected our hand baggage, and in due course set off for York. We had to wait a while there, and spent the time in getting lunch; and while we ate and drank we discussed our plans – or, rather, Frank and I listened to Kimberley explaining his.

"I take it," he said, "that the man who was with Lomas on the evening of the murder is a Leeds man. His postcard was written from Leeds; his old trench-coat bears the label of a Leeds tailor. That landlord at the railway hotel at Wilmoor Junction who said he felt certain that he'd seen this man somewhere before thought that if he had seen him it was probably on some racecourse: very likely the man is of the sporting fraternity. Well, there'll be means of finding out something in Leeds about the gentlemen of that kidney – they'll form a small group amongst themselves in the midst of a big and otherwise occupied population. Somebody may even be able to identify this trench-coat! We're doing very well, gentlemen!"

"I'd like to know your theory as to what happened that night?" said Frank. "You've got one, of course."

But Kimberley shook his head.

"I'd rather not say, sir," he replied. "I could put half a dozen theories before you, all plausible, and very likely all wrong. What I feel is that we must find Lomas and we must find the man who was with Lomas that night. At present the man seems to be the easiest fox to follow. Let us press after him, first. Lomas appears to have made himself scarce very successfully – I'm afraid he may have already got clean out of the country. But this other man, in all probability, hasn't the remotest notion that anybody knows anything about him. That's all in our favour. If a man who's wanted thinks himself absolutely secure he's within an ace of capture – he takes risks that the man who's afraid is careful not to take. If this chap is really a Leeds man, or known in Leeds, I think we shall unearth him – anyhow, I know a colleague in the detective force in Leeds who'll help, and we'll see him as soon as we get there."

We were in Leeds by three o'clock that afternoon, and Kimberley immediately led us to the police-headquarters and after introducing himself asked for a certain Detective-Sergeant Borlace. Borlace was at hand and presently came to us – a rotund, cheery-faced little man who gave Kimberley a surprised and almost affectionate greeting.

"And what brings you into these regions, my lad?" he asked. "Last man in the world I expected to see!"

"A matter that requires a good deal of explanation, old man!" replied Kimberley. "But I'll put it all as plainly and briefly as I can. You know, of course, all about what the newspapers are calling the Yorkshire Moorland Murder – that affair near Rievesley?"

"All?" said Borlace, with a shrug of his shoulders. "No! – I know what there's been in the papers: no more. Not in our district, that. But what of it – you aren't in it?"

"I am!" replied Kimberley. "And getting deeper in it. Now listen – because we've come here to Leeds on a definite clue, and I want some help – your help, to start with. I'll tell you all I know and what I've found out so far." He went on to narrate briefly the story of our recent discoveries, and finally showed Borlace the postcard and the trench-coat. "Now," he concluded, "You've been here in Leeds some time, to my knowledge – do you know anything of the man I'm wanting to find? Does that description suggest anybody to you? I reckon you know all the crooks and shady characters in this city?"

Borlace shook his head doubtfully.

"Tall, spare, dark man with a slight cast in his eye, very smartly dressed except for that thing?" he said, pointing to the disreputable trench-coat. "No! Can't say I do, Kim. But – you think he may be a sporting man?"

"The landlord at Wilmoor that I mentioned to you said he felt sure he'd seen this man before," replied Kimberley. "And if he had, he said, he felt equally sure it was on some racecourse or other."

Borlace thought awhile.

"Where are you staying?" he asked suddenly. "Hotel?"

"Don't know the place at all," replied Kimberley. "Suggest one."

"Go to the Queen's, by the Midland Station," said Borlace. "I'll come there tonight after dinner and bring with me a man – Detective-Sergeant Ample – who knows every racecourse, racing man, crook, tipster – all the fry – in the North of England. I'll tell him all you've told me before I bring him, and explain what you want; he'll probably take you to Costello's Corner."

"And what's Costello's Corner?" asked Kimberley.

"Costello's Corner," replied Borlace, with a laugh, "is a place worth visiting."

Chapter Sixteen

COSTELLO'S CORNER

BORLACE came to us at the Queen's Hotel that evening, bringing with him the man he had spoken of – a sharp-eyed, wide-awake sort of person, who, it seemed to me as I sat watching him while Kimberley talked, was either considerably puzzled or was racking his brains in the effort to awaken some temporarily lost chord of memory. Eventually – a whisky-and-soda and a cigar having failed to revive his recollections – he shook his head.

"Can't place him!" he said. "If he's anybody who's ever come under my observation at any time I ought to know him from your description – tall, spare chap, dark hair and complexion and slight cast in his eye – but there's the fact! I don't."

"No recollection of ever coming across him on any of these North-country racecourses?" asked Kimberley.

"No! And I know them all – from Doncaster to Newcastle. Still – of course – I know Lomas."

"You do?" exclaimed Kimberley.

"Well enough! Squire Lomas, as he's known. Seen him a hundred times at various race-meetings. About all he was good for, I should say. Bit of a waster – and kept some queer company."

"But you never remember seeing him with a man who answers to our description of this fellow we want?"

"I don't! Seen Lomas with, as I say, some queer company. Blacklegs, and that sort. But not with your man."

"Where did you see Lomas last?"

Our new ally considered this question for a minute or two; he was evidently a man who did not care to make a statement or give an opinion without reflection.

"Well," he replied at last, "I should say it would be at Thirsk Races – early in October. Yes – now I come to think of it, I did see Lomas there."

"That," remarked Borlace, "would be in his own district – not so many miles from his place. Kimberley," he added, turning to the newcomer in explanation, "doesn't know Yorkshire at all. That's why he wants the help of somebody like you, Ample, who does, and who also knows the racing fraternity."

"What grounds have you for believing this man you're after to belong to that lot?" asked Ample.

"None – except what the landlord at the inn at Wilmoor Junction said," replied Kimberley. "That he felt sure he'd seen the man before, somewhere, and that it must have been on a racecourse."

"Big order," muttered Ample. "Tens of thousands of people go to race-meetings whom you couldn't class as belonging to the racing fraternity. If this chap were a bookmaker, now – or a well-known punter – or a man who makes a regular point of following the turf, I'd know him. But let's go to Costello's Corner."

Kimberley repeated the question he had previously put to Borlace. What was Costello's Corner? The two men smiled.

"You'll see when you get there," said Ample. "But I may as well tell you. It's a bar, saloon, drinking-shop, whatever you like to call it, outwardly highly respectable, and very smart and up-to-date, kept by a certain Jim Costello, an Irishman, at the corner of two principal streets. And it's the nightly resort of all the so-called sportsmen of the city and neighbourhood – racing men, billiard players, pigeon-shooters, professional footballers, and so on, with a sprinkling of music-hall folk and their satellites. Odd crowd – but we might hear something. I know all the regular habitués there."

"Do they know you for what you are?" asked Kimberley, smiling.

"Lord bless you, yes – and Borlace too. What matter? Come on – we'll go round and I'll see if I can spot anybody who might give us a bit of information of the sort you're wanting."

Frank and I followed the three detectives out into the still-busy streets and left them to talk among themselves. We were having queer adventures, and I, personally, was doubtful as to anything resulting – it seemed to me that if Lomas and the unknown man had engaged in any secret conspiracy relating to Dr. Essenheim they would have done so in such a fashion as to make their own retreat entirely successful; in my opinion, they were both clear of the country and would never be heard of again. Still, there was no reason in trying anything, and all we could do was to follow our present leaders. So for the moment we followed into Costello's Corner.

Costello's Corner, outwardly, was, as Ample had said, a highly respectable-looking place – a saloon bar set at the corner of two good streets and having entrances from both. Following our guide and passing various small rooms or bars, called, I believe, in that part of the country by the appropriate name of Snugs, we presently found ourselves in a large and handsomely-fitted room, having a long bar down one side of it, presided over by half a dozen young ladies, carefully selected for their charms and appearance, and furnished liberally with plush-covered lounges and chairs and ornamented with mirrors, sporting prints, and trophies of the chase in the form of foxes' masks, stags' antlers, and stuffed specimens of the anglers' skill. The room was full of men and women and cigar smoke, and the chatter of voices and ring of glass was confusing to quiet persons like myself. At first I saw no corner into which one could sink, but Ample, who evidently knew everybody and whom everybody evidently knew, judging by the nods and salutations on all sides, steered us, as a party, into an alcove at one end of the place, and beckoned to a waiter.

"Better have something for the good of the house, as they say," he muttered. "Give it a name, gentlemen."

We sat there with our glasses and pipes or cigars for some little time, watching. The three detectives whispered amongst themselves: Frank and I sat silent, observing and wondering when anything was going to happen. Ten, fifteen, twenty minutes went by – then Ample suddenly started into activity. A little, elderly man, with the face of a comedian, and dressed in a suit of loud checks, came along; Ample hailed him as he was passing.

"Hullo, Jimmie," he called. "Here – a minute!"

The little man turned, saw who it was that had hailed him, and grinned as he came up to our table.

"Hullo, Mr. Ample," he said. "Wanting me? What is it this time? Burglary? Arson? Kidnapping? – or what? I see you've got a good lot of help with you!"

"Sit down, Jimmie, and have a drink," retorted Ample. He waved a hand towards the rest of us. "Friends o' mine,

Jimmie, all nice fellows. Gentlemen, Mr. Jimmie Wardleby, the cleverest professional tipster in the North of England. Now Jimmie, crowd in by me – I want you to do me a good turn."

The little man squeezed himself into a seat between Ample and Borlace and looked round at the rest of us with a knowing wink.

"Mr. Ample knows my good nature, gentlemen," he said. "It's my weak point, and he takes advantage of it. But your good health, Mr. Ample – and everybody's." He suddenly sat up in his chair, altered the expression of his face to one of judicial solemnity, and turned on his companion with a corresponding severity of tone. "And what can I do for you, sir?" he demanded.

"You can listen!" said Ample. "And be serious, Jimmie, my lad, for this is a serious matter – maybe a hanging matter for somebody! I want to give you a description of a certain man and to know if, from that description, you can say definitely if you know anything of him. It's not much of a description, unfortunately – it all comes in a few words. A tall, spare man, dark eyes and hair, and has a slight cast in one eye – "

The little man suddenly laid an arresting hand on Ample's arm.

"Stop there!" he exclaimed. "I know him!"

"You do? Good business, Jimmie! Who is he?"

But Jimmie shook his head vigorously.

"Ask me another, Mr. Ample! I don't know that! But I've seen the man you describe. Decided cast in his eye – I should call it a bad squint!"

"Well, where have you seen him?"

"I've seen him two or three times this last season. As far as I can remember, at York, and at Doncaster, and, I believe, at Newmarket. And I certainly saw him at Thirsk. He was talking to Squire Lomas."

Ample gave the rest of us a look. But nobody spoke, and he turned his attention once more to the tipster.

"Oh, you know Squire Lomas, do you?" he asked.

"Of course I do, Mr. Ample! Known him ever since he started chucking his money away!"

"And you're sure you saw this man with him at Thirsk?"

"Yes, I'm sure of that. I spoke to Mr. Lomas as I passed them. It struck me then that I'd seen the squinting chap before – at the places I mentioned."

"But you don't know who he is, nor what he is?"

"I don't, Mr. Ample. No idea."

"You don't think he's a bookmaker?"

"Oh, no, I'm sure he isn't. I should have known him."

"Jimmie goes all over England," explained Ample. "He knows every racecourse there is, and has been on all of 'em – not excepting Newmarket Heath! Well, Jimmie, another question. Does this man look like a well-to-do chap?"

"Very smart appearance, Mr. Ample. Bit over-dressed, if anything. Like me! But then, of course, I've got to draw attention to myself!"

"Of course, Jimmie, of course! Well, will you do something for me and my friends here? We want to find that man! We want – his evidence. Will you try to get me some more information about him? – on the quiet? You know where to bring it – or you'll be seeing me here."

The little man nodded a ready assent.

"I will, Mr. Ample!" he responded. "You once did me a rare good turn, and I'm only too glad to do you one – or try to. But – slow and soft is the word, Mr. Ample! I can make enquiries, but" – he waved a hand towards the miscellaneous assemblage before us – "you know what sort these are! Guarded – guarded! That's the word too, Mr. Ample – guarded and judicious enquiry. Leave it to me, sir, I'll let you know if and when I find anything out."

We left Costello's Corner a few minutes later, and after taking leave of the two local detectives, returned to our hotel. Kimberley – I was beginning to regard him as being a good deal of an incurable optimist – appeared to be quite satisfied with the evening's proceedings and results.

"That little beggar will find out something," he said, with a chuckle. "And he'll report to Ample, and Ample will report to me. We'll go for London tomorrow morning, gentlemen, I think. But before going, I'll just show that trench-coat to the tailors here whose name it bears – Kersey and Sadwell. I noticed their place of business in one of the streets we passed through."

He got the parcel containing the trench-coat from Borlace next morning, and we all three went out to Kersey & Sadwell with it. This was obviously a high-class tailoring business, and the partner who came out to us, on receipt of Kimberley's card, was a superior sort of man who, scenting a mystery, conducted us into a private office. He listened with deep attention to what Kimberley had to say. And so did Frank and I – for Kimberley did not say where he had found the coat nor that a certain suspicion attached to it. He merely said that in the course of a criminal investigation this coat had come into his hands, and that, as it bore the label of Messrs. Kersey & Sadwell, he had come to them to ascertain if they could tell him anything about it.

"Of course, all this is in strict confidence," he concluded. "Anything you can tell me, Mr. – "

"I am Mr. Sadwell," said the tailor. He was examining the label inside the coat – a label stitched in behind the collar – and after a close glance at it he laid the coat aside. "I can tell you to whom we sold this trench-coat, Inspector," he said. "It would be, of course, to a customer of ours, so – this is in confidence, eh?"

"Strict confidence, sir, at present," replied Kimberley. "No use will be made of any information you give me without your permission."

Sadwell turned to a row of ledgers or memorandum books which stood ranged along a shelf in the office. He took one down, turned over its pages, and presently closed the book again with a decisive snap.

"This coat was sold, three years ago, to Mr. Hird Lomas of Harlesden Hall," he said.

"Mr. Lomas used to be a customer – a very good customer – of ours. Of late – the last twelve months or so we haven't seen him. This any use to you, Inspector?"

"It may be of the greatest use, sir," replied Kimberley. He packed up his parcel again, thanked Mr. Sadwell, and we went away. "I understand things now," he remarked, as we went back to our hotel. "That unknown man turned up at Wilmoor Junction without an overcoat! Lomas had this old trench-coat in his car – he lent it to the man. But – which of 'em was wearing it when... oh, well, that'll come later, Gentlemen, let's get the next express to town – we'll pursue matters there, or from there."

While Frank went into the hotel with Kimberley to collect the things and settle the bill, I turned into the adjacent station to find out when we could get a train. Chancing to glance at the bookstall as I passed it, I saw that the London papers had just come in, and bought a copy of *The Times*. A few minutes later, having ascertained that an express left for St. Pancras in half an hour, I strolled across to the hotel, opening *The Times* as I walked. And suddenly, on a middle page, I saw something which there and then sent me hurrying, amazed and excited, in search of my companions.

Chapter Seventeen

IS IT THE SAME?

CONSIDERING the nature of the enquiry in which we were engaged, it is little wonder that what I read in *The Times* was enough to make me halt, dead, in the middle of a crowded street. Another glance at the – to me – startling paragraph, and I dashed through the traffic and burst into the hotel, where I found Frank and Kimberley ready to go across to the train.

"Look at this – look at this!" I exclaimed, spreading the newspaper on a table before them. "What do you make of that, now?"

They stared at me and then at the paragraph I indicated. I, too, read it once more, wondering.

> *Amongst the rarer items to be offered by Messrs. Saddleworths at their next sale is a copy of the exceedingly rare first edition of Bunyan's Pilgrim's Progress. This, described as being in unusually good condition, and as the property of a lady, has only recently been discovered amongst the odds and ends of a private library. Perfect copies of*

the first edition are so very scarce (there are said to be only some six or seven known to experts in bibliography) that there will doubtless be keen competition amongst collectors for this particular one. Additional interest attaches to its appearance on the market from the fact that another copy came into prominence not long ago in connection with the murder of the famous bibliophile, Dr. Essenheim, who was believed to have had it in his pocket when he met his death at a lonely spot on the Yorkshire Moors. That copy, of course, has not been heard of since, and up to now all efforts to trace it have been as fruitless as the quest for Dr. Essenheim's assailant. The copy about to be offered by Messrs. Saddleworths, has, fortunately, a clear history behind it.

We all turned and glanced at each other. There was a moment's silence; then Kimberley spoke:

"A clear history behind it, eh?" he said. "Um – well, we'll have to enquire into the truth of that! Saddleworths? First-class people, to be sure, are Saddleworths – tip-toppers in their line of business. But Saddleworths may have been taken in."

"You're already suspecting that this is our copy?" suggested Frank.

"Why, it's certainly a bit queer that a copy should turn up at Saddleworths so soon after our copy's been stolen," answered Kimberley. "The only thing is – is it likely that whoever stole his copy from Dr. Essenheim's dead body would be so rash as to put it on the market within such a short time? We've always believed at headquarters, as I've told you more than once, that the book would turn up again, but our notion was that it would be across the Atlantic. And, of course, this may be another instance of what a lot of coincidence there is in things! Still, we've got to see this Saddleworth book. These things are generally on view at Saddleworths a few days before their sales, but we can't wait for that. What time does our train go, Captain?"

"We've a quarter of an hour," I replied.

"Then come across to the telegraph office in the station and we'll wire Mr. Heddleston to meet us at St. Pancras," said Kimberley. "He's the man to take this job in hand, as being the late Dr. Essenheim's solicitor. We'll get him to go with us at once to Saddleworths as soon as we reach town."

We went over to the station, wired to Heddleston, and got into the express. And during most of the time of our journey we talked of nothing but this new development, discussing what it meant, or, rather, what it might mean. Personally, the more I thought of it, the more I felt inclined to believe that the thing was a coincidence, though a very unusual and remarkable one. I couldn't bring myself to believe that Dr. Essenheim's murderer would dare to produce the very article for the possession of which he had committed a double crime, so soon. I put this view of it before my companions. Kimberley shook his head.

"Yes," he said. "But if this is the copy we're concerned about – the placing of it in Saddleworths' hands may be another piece of barefaced bluff – we can guess on whose part! And mind you, gentlemen, if it is, it'll have been worked out with rare skill – it'll be the result of a very carefully designed and executed plot." He picked up a copy of *The Times* which lay on our table in the luncheon car and began to turn it over. "I don't see any advertisement of Saddleworths in here to-day," he remarked. "We might have learnt a bit more if there'd been one."

"Saddleworths' advertisements of forthcoming sales are generally in *The Times Literary Supplement*," I said. "I'll see if I can get one, next stop."

The next – our first – stop was at Sheffield, and there I managed to get what I wanted and turned at once to the back page.

"Here it is!" I said, laying the paper before the others. "But it only tells what we know already. The book's mentioned as the property of a lady. Nothing more. Can we insist on knowing who the lady is?"

Kimberley shook his head and grew thoughtful.

"I don't know where we stand, exactly, gentlemen," he said. "From what little I know about Saddleworths, I believe you can go in there a few days before a sale and inspect the books they're going to offer at auction. Well, supposing we go there and inspect this particular copy of old Bunyan? We can't say to Saddleworth, point blank, 'Look here, who's the lady who's given you this copy to sell – out with her name!' We could, of course, ask that, putting it in polite language, but Saddleworths wouldn't tell us, any more than a banker would tell you how much Dick Jones or Tom Robinson has in the bank, or a lawyer divulge what's in Jack Brown's will! If we could go to Saddleworths, inspect the copy, and then say, 'That copy of *The Pilgrim's Progress* is the copy stolen from the dead body of Dr. Essenheim and you've got to account for your present possession of it!' that, ah, that would be a very different matter! But – we can't!"

"Why can't we?" growled Frank.

"Well, sir, I reckon you know more about this old book trade than I do," replied Kimberley, "but, as far as my limited knowledge goes, one copy of an edition is very much, or, rather, just the same in appearance to what all other copies of that edition are! How are you going to tell one from t'other? If they're all printed alike and bound alike – and especially if, as I'm given to understand this book is – of considerable age, how are you going to distinguish between them?"

"Copies vary," said Frank. "One might be – as this is said to be – in fine condition; another might be practically worn out."

"Just so!" agreed Kimberley. "But that's a question of degree! As far as I can remember, from what you've told me and what I've read, the Lomas copy of this old book was a very fine one – in an excellent state of preservation. Well, this copy advertised by Saddleworths is said to be the same! Who's going to differentiate between 'em? The difficulty is here, gentlemen – we know of nobody who can positively identify the Lomas copy even if we ourselves felt sure we were looking at it. There are only three people we know of who could swear to it. One's Dr. Essenheim, and he, poor gentleman, is gone! Another's Lomas – and where the devil is Lomas? The third is that chap Lomas had with him – and he's having the devil's own game with us!"

"You've forgotten a fourth man," said Frank. "Whiteley!"

Kimberley started.

"You're right, sir!" he exclaimed penitently. "I'd forgotten Whiteley! Whiteley did see the Lomas copy, didn't he? It was Whiteley who advised Lomas to write to Dr. Essenheim about it, wasn't it? Good! – we must call in Whiteley to help us. But first let's see what Mr. Heddleston can do for us at Saddleworths."

Heddleston, curious and impatient, was waiting for us at St. Pancras, and we took him into a quiet corner of the smoking-room in the hotel to tell him our news – a brief question to him on our first greeting showed that the paragraph in *The Times* had escaped his notice. And on reading it he immediately shook his head.

"No!" he said, with emphasis. "No – no! I can't believe that's our copy! It's a strange, almost unbelievable

149

coincidence. I can't conceive that any man would be such a fool as to take to Saddleworths a famous book for the possession of which he'd murdered and robbed another man! It's altogether too soon to expect that Lomas copy to come into the limelight again, and when it does it won't be here!"

"Well, anyway, Mr. Heddleston, you'll go with us to Saddleworths?" asked Kimberley. "We ought to see this copy of theirs, you know."

"Oh, certainly, we'll go to Saddleworths," agreed Heddleston. "They know me there, and I'll get hold of a responsible man who'll give us full information. It's really a very remarkable coincidence," he went on, as we left the hotel to seek a taxi-cab, "but I feel sure it is a coincidence. Why, the man who took the Lomas copy from Dr. Essenheim's body would simply be putting his head in a noose to bring it into view so soon after his crime! Incredible!"

"There's such a thing as bluff, sir," remarked Kimberley. "And we're dealing with some very cunning rogues, in my opinion. I hope you'll be able to persuade Saddleworths to give us every bit of information they possess."

"Oh, yes, yes!" said Heddleston. "I've no doubt about that!"

But when it came to interviewing the responsible person at Saddleworths of whom Heddleston had spoken so confidently, I began to see that not even Heddleston was going to get particulars which Saddleworths were not in a position to give, or were not allowed to give. There was no difficulty about seeing and even handling the book – there it lay before us, a queer little volume for which the unlearned in such matters wouldn't have given five hundred farthings, let alone five thousand pounds, but as to narrating its recent history, and, as it were, setting out its title-deeds, no!

"The property of a lady!" said the representative, with a snap of the lips which showed us that we should be wise not to ask too many questions.

"May I know her name?" asked Heddleston.

The representative smiled, acidly.

"I fear not. Our client wishes to remain in the background."

"Final?" said Heddleston.

"As far as we're concerned – yes!"

"Well," continued Heddleston. "You have my card, so you know who I am. This is Inspector Kimberley, of Scotland Yard. This is Mr. Frank Essenheim, nephew of Dr. Essenheim, the famous American bibliophile, whom you, of course, know well enough. This is Captain Mannering, who was Dr. Essenheim's secretary at the time of his murder. Now, you are doubtless aware – "

Before Heddleston could say more, the representative of the Saddleworth firm cut in, with a smile.

"Yes, I know what you're going to say, Mr. Heddleston," he said. "And that is that when Dr. Essenheim was murdered he had on him a copy of the first edition of *The Pilgrim's Progress* which he had just bought from a Mr. Hird Lomas, of Harlesden Hall, in Yorkshire. The murderer or murderers stole that copy. Of course, we know all that – it was in all the papers. And now you're wondering if this copy is that! – isn't that it?"

"I didn't say so," retorted Heddleston. "I asked – To whom does this copy belong?"

"And I answered that it is the property of a lady – whose name we are not at liberty to tell you, or anyone," replied the other, good-humouredly. "We ourselves know its history, anyway!"

"And you're satisfied about it?" asked Heddleston.

"We shouldn't be dealing with it if we weren't!"

"You know your client?"

"We know our client – sufficiently well, anyhow."

Heddleston looked at Kimberley. Kimberley was looking hard at the book, and his face showed nothing.

"Oh, well – "said Heddleston, irresolutely. "I suppose – "

Frank put himself forward from the second row.

"Look here!" he said. "Between now and the sale, I guess you'll allow any responsible person to see that book?"

"Certainly, Mr. Essenheim, just as you've seen it!"

"And to examine it?"

"Certainly!"

"You'll make no objection if I bring an expert here?"

Our informant smiled.

"Bring a dozen if you like, Mr. Essenheim," he said. "We shan't mind! The greater publicity, the more we shall get for our client."

Frank nodded, and, turning on his heel, walked out into the street, the rest of us following.

"Look here!" he said. "We've got to wire straight away to that man Whiteley, asking him to come here right now!"

"Whiteley?" exclaimed Heddleston. "What – "

"Whiteley," I said, "is the only man who can positively identify the Lomas copy; Lomas has gone! But Whiteley made a careful examination of the book before ever Lomas approached Dr. Essenheim about its sale. If that copy we've just seen is the Lomas copy – "

"Can't believe it is!" muttered Heddleston. "Incredible! Still – "

"If it is, Whiteley will know," I said. "We must have Whiteley! He – "

"Here's a post-office," interrupted Frank. "Come in with me, Mannering. Heddleston's half asleep," he muttered, as we went in. "But I guess I'm waking up! Now let's word this thing in a way that'll make Whiteley run for the next train."

Late that night Whiteley walked in upon us at the Carlton Hotel.

Chapter Eighteen

IDENTIFIED

WE had said no more in our wire to Whiteley than that we believed the Lomas copy of *The Pilgrim's Progress* had come to light and that we wanted him, Lomas not being available, to come and identify it, and we now had to tell him all about our recent discoveries and our visit to Saddleworths. He smiled on hearing of the auctioneer's assurances.

"Maybe!" he said. "But it's a somewhat astonishing coincidence if this really is another copy of the first edition! First editions – genuine and undoubted – of *The Pilgrim's Progress* are not like blackberries, to be picked up anywhere. However, if this is the Lomas copy, I shall know at one glance!"

"You can speak positively as to that?" I asked.

"Positively! With absolute certainty," he answered. "You can be at ease on that point."

"How will you know it's the Lomas copy?" demanded Frank.

Whiteley gave us a knowing look.

"Because I put a mark on it!" he replied. "My private mark. Lomas left it with me for an hour or two that day he brought it to my place at York, and as I thought there might at some time or other be reasons for my being able to identify it – you never know – I put my private mark, in pencil, on the margin of one of the pages." He drew out a pocket-book and referred to something. "The mark is on page 33," he added. "It's a mere pencilling – but it's mine."

Frank let out an exclamation of satisfaction and then shook his head – not, evidently, in any doubt, but with a meaning.

"It isn't that I want merely to recover the book!" he said. "What I want – if this is the copy – is to get at those devils through it. If we can only do that – "

"Lomas," remarked Whiteley, "would appear to have clean gone. Nothing has been heard of him, in our parts, anyway. That is, as to his recent whereabouts. I heard a queer story about him, though, the other day, which may throw some light on his recent doings. You know, or you mayn't know, that there has been a certain amount of speculation in the newspapers – local papers – as to Lomas' whereabouts. Well, there's a man I know well in York who, discussing this with me one day last week, told me something about Lomas. This man, I may say, is a money-lender, but quite a decent chap. Lomas some time ago got a loan out of him and never repaid it, nor, indeed, the interest on it. The lender eventually sued him and got judgment against him. Eventually, as Lomas did nothing, he told him that he'd have to have the judgment enforced – by execution, I suppose. Well, that was not long before Lomas came to me with his *Pilgrim's Progress* – I compared dates carefully I may tell you, when I heard this story. When the man threatened Lomas with execution Lomas said he'd no money: the man replied that he'd wait a fortnight to give Lomas a chance of doing, at any rate, something. Within that fortnight Lomas suddenly turned up at his creditor's office in York and satisfied the debt and costs in full! Every penny!"

"How much?" asked Frank.

"Oh – somewhere between four and five hundred pounds. But that's not the point. The point is – where had he got that money. Now, by a very careful comparison of dates I came to a certain conclusion. This – the settling-up with his money-lending creditor – occurred between Lomas' coming to me with his *Pilgrim's Progress* and his final disposing of it to Dr. Essenheim. Now then, does anything suggest itself to you two young gentlemen?"

Nothing suggested itself to me, and Frank shook his head.

"Well, something suggests itself to me!" said Whiteley with a knowing smile. "And I shall be surprised if my idea's not correct – that is, if we ever do get at the real truth of this business. I think that after Lomas had been to me with his book, and had got my professional opinion, as an expert – you must remember I gave him my opinion in that capacity, formally written out, saying that I set down the value of the book at, at any rate, three or four thousand pounds – he went off somewhere and raised ready money on it! Just that!"

"What! – by pawning it?" I asked.

"Not pawning – no. Perhaps he left it as security – not with a pawnbroker – together with my letter," replied Whiteley. "Or, more likely still, considering what we know, he sold a share in it – a half-share, or a one-third, or a quarter. We know now, from what you've found out, that Lomas told Dr. Essenheim that he had a partner in the proprietorship of this book – doesn't that bear out my suggestion? Well, I think that partner was the man whom Lomas met at Wilmoor Junction and concerning whom you've discovered certain facts. That man, without doubt, acquired a certain interest in the book, and, in consequence, claimed and exercised his right to be present at Harlesden Hall when the book was sold to Dr. Essenheim. Indeed, I think there was another good reason for his presence there! I think he brought the book with him!"

"You mean that if Lomas raised ready money from him, he left the book in his hands?" I suggested.

"Just that! I think he kept the book until Lomas sent for him to come with it at a certain hour and day to meet Dr. Essenheim," replied Whiteley. "That, at any rate, is my theory. If it's correct, it explains a great deal that you've brought to light in your recent investigations. Now the first thing to do is to make sure whether this copy at Saddleworths is really Lomas' copy or not. If it's not – well, it's a remarkable thing that two perfect copies of so rare a book should turn up about the same time; if it is – "

He paused there, shaking his head and smiling.

"Well, if it is – ?" I said.

"If it is," he continued, "well, if it is, then I suppose you will want to know a good deal about... the lady! Who is she?"

"Saddleworths say it's against their rules to divulge the names of their principals," I remarked.

"Saddleworths," said Whiteley, "can say what they please! But Saddleworths cannot do what they please when it comes to a question of disputed ownership." He turned to Frank. "This Lomas copy was sold to Dr. Essenheim for five thousand pounds," he continued. "It was his property when he died. To whom, Mr. Essenheim, did your uncle leave his estate, real and personal – in other words, who's got what he left?"

"I have!" replied Frank. "He left me, unreservedly, everything he had. Heddleston has his will – or a copy of it. The will itself is in New York."

"Very well, you're the owner of this book," said Whiteley. "So your path's plainly marked for you. If I can prove, tomorrow morning – no, by Jove, this morning, for it's well past midnight – that the copy at Saddleworths is the very identical copy which Lomas exhibited to me at York, and, therefore, the copy sold by Lomas to your uncle, you can at once get an injunction against Saddleworths, the effect of which would be to prevent them from selling it until its ownership had been settled. But Heddleston will put you up to all that – I suppose he'll go with us to Saddleworths in the morning?"

Heddleston, of course, went with us to Saddleworths early that day, and having been duly posted in all that Whiteley had said to us at our midnight conference, he acted as spokesman when we were admitted to the presence of the representative of the firm whom we had seen the previous afternoon and who was, in fact, the managing partner.

"We have brought Mr. Whiteley to see the copy of *The Pilgrim's Progress* which you showed us yesterday," began Heddleston. "Mr. Whiteley is – "

The managing partner smiled and waved a hand.

"We know Mr. Whiteley well enough!" he interrupted. "Mr. Whiteley is, on occasion, a well-known figure in our sales-room. Mr. Whiteley wants to see the copy about which we were talking yesterday? Very good – but. . .for some special reason?"

"Mr. Whiteley had in his hands – and for a short time in his possession – the copy of *The Pilgrim's Progress* which Mr. Hird Lomas sold to Dr. Essenheim and which was stolen from Dr. Essenheim's dead body," answered Heddleston.

"We are strongly of opinion that the copy which you showed us yesterday may be that copy – Mr. Whiteley can say definitely if it is!"

The managing partner and Whiteley exchanged glances.

"How can you prove as much as that, Mr. Whiteley?" asked the managing partner.

"Supposing this is the copy in question – what proof can you give? I mean, of course, absolute proof."

"I'll tell you," replied Whiteley. "When Lomas found his copy of the book at Harlesden Hall he brought it to me in York to inspect. He left it with me for an hour or two. While it was with me I placed my private mark in it – on the left-hand margin of a certain page – "

"Your private mark is – what?" asked the managing partner.

"It is the minuscule form of the Greek letter Phi," replied Whiteley, "which, as you are probably aware, is a lateral oval with a slightly sloping stroke running upward through it from left at the bottom to right at the top. I'll make it for you – exactly as I make it in any book which I mark for purposes of my own."

He seized a scrap of paper and taking a pencil from his pocket made the mark:

"Now," he continued, "we can put the matter to a definite test in a moment. If you will get your copy and open it – none of us, if you please, will touch it – and will turn to a certain page I shall mention, you will see at once whether my mark is there or not!"

The managing partner rose from his desk, unlocked a safe, and turned to us with the small, insignificant-looking volume in his hand. He looked at Whiteley.

"Well?" he said. "What page?"

"Page 33 – the left-hand margin – in a light pencil mark," said Whiteley.

I think we all held our breath for the next few seconds. The managing partner opened the book and took one glance at the place indicated. His face fell.

"The mark is there!" he said.

For a moment nobody spoke. Then Whiteley gave a dry cough.

"I never doubted that it would be!" he remarked cynically. "It would be too much to expect two copies of such an exceedingly rare find as that to appear at one time. Coincidence is coincidence, but – " he shrugged his shoulders and turned to Heddleston. "You know now!" he said. "That's the Lomas copy!"

Heddleston glanced at the managing partner, who was obviously considerably disturbed by Whiteley's positive declaration.

"What do you propose to do?" he enquired. "This book is undoubtedly the copy of *The Pilgrim's Progress* bought from Mr. Lomas by Dr. Essenheim, stolen from Dr. Essenheim at the time of his death, his murder, and now the property of his nephew, Mr. Frank Essenheim, whom you see here. But what we want to know is – From whom did you receive it? Who is the lady?"

The managing partner suddenly reached for a newspaper which lay carelessly thrown on his desk.

"That's got out!" he said. "How it got out, I don't know – it hasn't got out from here. Read it for yourselves."

We crowded together to read a paragraph marked in blue pencil in one of the popular morning newspapers:

> *WE understand that the very rare copy of the first edition of Bunyan's Pilgrim's Progress, shortly to be sold at Saddleworths, is the property of Miss Cissie Frayne, one of our most promising danseuses, who discovered it under romantic circumstances. We hope to give Miss Frayne's own account of her lucky find in our next issue.*

"Well?" said Heddleston, laying the paper down and still insistent. "Who is this girl?" The managing partner spread his hands.

"I don't understand this at all!" he said. "The young woman, a very well-behaved, modest, quietly-dressed girl, brought this book to me with a perfectly straightforward story. She said that recently an elderly neighbour of the family, to whom she had shown some little attention in her last illness, had left her various matters, including a box full of old books. In looking these over she had found – this! Her attention had been attracted to it by having recently read about the Essenheim case – and so she brought it to us, on the advice of her clergyman. Of course, having regard to what Mr. Whiteley says, I must get her here. In the meantime, Mr. Heddleston, the book shall be locked up and no one shall touch or even see it."

We went out – to consult. And then, for the first time that morning, Kimberley, to whom we had telephoned to meet us outside Saddleworth's office, and who had been a deeply-interested spectator of our interview with the managing partner, became vocal.

"You saw what was in that newspaper paragraph, gentlemen?" he said. "It meant that this girl, Miss Cissie Frayne, is being interviewed on behalf of the paper. Well, what one interviewer can do, another can do! I suggest, as a practical thing, that you, Mr. Frank, and you, Captain Mannering, pretend to be newspaper men and go and get out of the young lady all you can! You're both good-looking fellows, and all you want is tact, diplomacy – "

Frank looked at me. And at what I saw in his face, I nodded. He turned to Heddleston.

"The address?" he said. "Get it, and we'll go right there!"

Heddleston dived into Saddleworths again and came back within the minute.

"The address," he said, "is 35, Battlement Street, Camden Town."

Chapter Nineteen

MISS CISSIE FRAYNE

KIMBERLEY drew Frank and myself aside: he was obviously brimming with eagerness. "Now, gentlemen," he said, "you can make a highly successful job of this if you go the right way about it. I know where this place is – Battlement Street – and I'll go up there with you and hang around while you call on this young lady: when you've seen her and got out of her all you can, we'll meet, and you can report progress. Go as representatives of American papers – say you're immensely interested in this remarkable find. Let Mr. Frank do most of the talking – that'll convince her that you're genuine Yankees. Be tactful – diplomatic – don't do anything, say anything, to excite her suspicions. But keep in view your real object – to find out from her where she got the book. Of course" – here Kimberley checked himself, looked thoughtful, and smiled – "of course, if my conception of the whole thing is correct, the young lady'll tell you a whole pack of lies! But never mind – swallow 'em – I'll help you to digest 'em, later! Now let's get a taxi and be off."

We hailed a passing cab and rode up to Camden Town. Battlement Street, which we approached carefully – on foot – proved to be one of the most respectable thoroughfares in that somewhat drab and dreary quarter: a street of undistinguished little houses, all built exactly alike, and nearly every one having a plant of some forbidding aspect standing in state on a small table between the dingy lace curtains of the ground floor front window. And at the corner was a pretentious-looking tavern, the Battlement Arms, to which Kimberley drew our attention.

"I'll watch you into the house," he said. "If she's at home, and you go in, I'll give you three-quarters of an hour to an hour. Then, when you come out, you'll find me somewhere round here. If you don't see me in the street, walk into that saloon bar. That, anyway, will be a good place to talk. Now, bear in mind all I suggested. And if you see the girl's telling you a lot of tarradiddles, keep your ears open and encourage her!"

We approached Number 35. I felt pretty much as I used to do when going over the top in Flanders. But Frank appeared to be quite cool; he looked, indeed, as if he were going to enjoy himself.

"I've been at this interviewing game before," he said, as we waited for a response to our knock. "Done a fine lot of newspaper work in my time, way over in Boston, years ago. I guess this is something out of the common, though. Look here! I represent the *Boston Morning Sentinel* – there isn't such a thing in existence, but that doesn't matter – and you're the European representative of the *San Francisco and Los Angeles Joint Mail* – that doesn't exist, either, nor does it matter that it doesn't."

"Well, you do the talking," said I. "I'm no hand at it."

"I reckon I'll do the questioning," he replied. "Well let her talk – if she will. But maybe there's nobody at home – "

Just then, however, the door opened – slightly. A girl looked out on us, through the very narrow opening. When she saw Frank, she smiled.

"Good morning," said Frank in his best manner. "Miss Frayne? – Miss Cissie Frayne? Have we the pleasure – "

"I'm not Miss Frayne," replied the girl, still smiling. "But Miss Frayne's in. Who shall I say – ?"

"This gentleman's the European representative of the San Francisco and Los Angeles Joint Mail, a very important newspaper," said Frank, gravely, "and I represent the Boston Morning Sentinel, one of the most influential journals in the United States. We've read of Miss Frayne's romantic discovery of *The Pilgrim's Progress*, and as our great book-collectors are immensely interested in such finds we'd like – "

I had been under the impression for quite thirty seconds that there was a second girl somewhere close behind the first, and that I had been right was proved by the sudden appearance of a vivacious-looking damsel whose yellow hair, blue eyes, and general aspect were of the type that one sees in plenty around the stage-doors when the pantomime season is on. She smiled widely – at Frank – and indicated a welcome.

"Oh, will you come in, please!" she said a little nervously. "I'm Miss Frayne, and I'm sure I don't know however that piece of news got into the paper this morning, for it didn't come from me, I can assure you. I've had a gentleman from that paper already to-day, but of course, he wouldn't tell me where they got this information. This way, if you please – this is my friend, Miss Georgina Sneppe. It's rather lucky you found us in just now, for as a rule we're away at rehearsals at this time, but we're out of an engagement temporarily, so we're at home. Of course, I don't know what I can have to say that would interest any American paper – I've never been interviewed by anybody before this morning – that other gentleman was the first."

We were in a shabby little parlour by this time, and I was able to inspect Miss Cissie Frayne and Miss Georgie Sneppe at my leisure. I should say Miss Frayne was five-and-twenty years old. As I have already recorded, she had yellow hair – I should say it had been transformed into yellow from some other hue – and blue eyes. She was fairly good-looking and fairly well attired, and she was somewhat nervous and somewhat gauche, and consequently talked very fast, punctuating her flow of language with little staccato laughs. As for Miss Sneppe, she was a dark-eyed damsel, younger and fresher than her friend, observant, watchful, and reserved of speech, and I saw that she was sizing Frank and myself up with great care.

"Enterprising of him!" said Frank. "Well, we came along as soon as ever we saw that paragraph. You see, there are no end of big men in our country that are just mad on this book-collecting game, and of course as soon as we read of your discovery we were keen to get some news, so that our people at home could read it." He ostentatiously produced a note-book and pencil, and I followed his example. "Now how did you come to find this very valuable old book, Miss Frayne?" he asked. Then, holding up a warning finger, he added, solemnly, "And don't you forget that the more romance – and publicity – there is given to it, the more money you'll get when those Saddleworth people auction it!"

"Do you think I shall?" said Miss Frayne.

"Oh, well, I'm getting quite excited – and a bit frightened – about it. How did I find it? Well, if you really want to know, I found it in that box!"

She pointed to a wooden box – the sort of thing in which chandlers pack candles, or grocers, soap – which stood in an alcove near the hearth, and appeared to be filled with a miscellaneous collection of old books, magazines, and illustrated papers. Frank glanced at it and then turned to me with a solemn face.

"It's a great pity we haven't got a camera with us," he said. "We'd have taken a photo of that box and Miss Frayne standing by it. What is it I see on it? Oh, 'Blenkin's Best Soft Soap,' eh? And you found the book in there?"

"In there!" declared Miss Frayne. "Right at the bottom of all the other old stuff you see there. It was this way – my friend and I have lived here (we have three ground floor rooms) for two or three years, and we know some of our neighbours, the more respectable ones. There was an old lady lived next door that I used to help a little when she was getting infirm – "

"It would be an advantage – give colour to the thing – if we knew her name," suggested Frank, lifting his pencil.

"Miss Cooke – that was her name Miss Henrietta Cooke. Well, she died, not very long ago, and she left me several little things, and amongst them that box, full of old books and papers. Of course, I'd no idea there was anything of value in that box, but one day I turned out what was there, and I came across this *Pilgrim's Progress*. Just fancy – quite by accident!"

"Well, I guess you didn't suspect it was of any value, eh?" suggested Frank. "An old, time-worn thing like that!"

Miss Frayne laughed. It was a quiet laugh – and there was a look of quiet slyness in her eyes when she replied.

"Well, I rather did!" she answered. "I did wonder if it mightn't be – very valuable!"

"Know something about old books, eh?" asked Frank.

"No, I don't! I don't know anything," admitted Miss Frayne candidly. "But, you see, I'd just been reading about that murder up in Yorkshire, on the moors – the murder of an American gentleman – "

"I know!" said Frank. "Read all about it, myself."

"Well, a rare copy of *The Pilgrim's Progress* was mentioned in connection with that," continued Miss Frayne. "I read in one paper that such a copy was probably worth thousands of pounds, so I wondered if mine would be worth anything. And so I showed it to a clergyman that I know near here, and he advised me to take it to Saddleworths so that they could sell it for me. And – I did! And that's all I can tell you. Do you think Saddleworths'll get me a lot of money for it?"

"Pity some of our big collectors are not across here at present," said Frank. "That one you mentioned just now – the Yorkshire moorland affair – he gave a pile for that copy you read about. That's never been heard of since – strange, isn't it? There are people who'd give a very handsome reward to anyone who could give information about that!"

Miss Georgie Sneppe, standing near the window and listening silently to all that was going on, turned towards Frank.

"What sort of reward?" she asked abruptly.

"I said – 'handsome'," replied Frank.

"What do you call 'handsome'?" she enquired. "Five pounds?"

"I know a man who would cheerfully pay five hundred pounds," said Frank. "And spot cash, too!" He turned from Miss Sneppe to Miss Frayne. "Very odd coincidence that you should find a copy about the same time that that other copy disappeared, wasn't it? Adds interest to the matter. I suppose you'll attend the auction of your property, Miss Frayne?"

"Oh, I suppose I shall – Georgie will have to go with me!" replied the fortunate owner. "Do you really think it will fetch a lot of money?"

Frank affected to consider matters.

"Well," he said, "I don't reckon to be a walking encyclopaedia on bibliographical matters, but I know a bit from what I've read. These copies of the very first edition of

The Pilgrim's Progress are very scarce indeed. I recollect what our own great authority, Dr. Rosenbach, says about 'em. He says that if one of the half-dozen perfect editions came on the market to-day it would likely fetch as much as between forty-five and fifty thousand dollars!"

"How much is that – in English money?" enquired Miss Frayne, innocently.

"Well, that's about between nine and ten thousand pounds," replied Frank. "Maybe yours is one of these perfect copies. If so you'll make a lot more money out of it than old man Bunyan ever did!"

"I don't know anything about the book market," observed Miss Frayne. "Me and Georgie are in the dancing line. But we're out of an engagement at present – we were in the ballet at the Floradolium last time."

Frank affected interest in his notes for a moment or two: so did I.

"Well!" he said after an interval, "Guess this'll write up very well, but can't you tell me a bit more about the history of this little old book, now? Say, what sort of lady was that old Miss Henny So-and-So – Cooke, was it? Old family, likely? Ain't there no family traditions to say something about? Book been in the Cooke family ever since great-great-great grandfather's time – and so on?"

"I never heard her mention the book," replied Miss Frayne. "You see, she just left various things to me and the book was amongst them. It was quite accidental, of course, that I found it. It didn't look to be anything valuable, you know – an old thing like that! Me, I shouldn't have given two pence for it! But then I'd read all about that murder in Yorkshire, you see, and I said to myself, 'Well,' I said, 'if the book that's mentioned there was valuable, mine must be.' And that's what the clergyman said. You should have seen him open his eyes – and his mouth – when I showed the book to him! Of course, he's got a lot of books of his own – beautiful books, a whole room full of them, all in lovely bindings. But I'll tell you what he said when I showed him my book: 'My dear!' he said, just like that, 'my dear, you see my library? Well, it cost me a good deal of money to get together, but if this is a genuine first edition,' he said, 'why, it's worth very likely ten times as much as all my books put together!' That's what he said – the Reverend Simpkinson, Vicar of St. Crucifige, round the corner."

"That's good copy," muttered Frank, busily writing. "We'll put that in. Now there's another little thing: we ought to have a good photo of yourself to put in the paper along with this. Got a good one – recent?"

Miss Frayne thought that she had, in her bedroom, and she left us, to fetch it. And as soon as she'd gone out of the room, Miss Sneppe advanced into the limelight.

"I say!" she said in a significant whisper "Is that true what you said – that somebody would give five hundred pounds to know something about – about that book that was stolen in Yorkshire? Is it – honest?"

"Sure thing!" said Frank. "Honest Injun! I know the man! But – why?"

Miss Sneppe laid a finger on her very red lips.

"H-sh!" she said. "Meet me by the Battlement Arms in half an hour and I'll tell you something. Careful!"

Miss Frayne came back with a photograph of herself. It was, she said, apologetically, in costume – which meant that there was a liberal display of Miss Frayne's charms of limb and figure, but little of Miss Frayne's under- or overwear – yet all she had. And, carrying this with us, we presently took leave of the two young ladies and went away – to find Kimberley in the saloon bar of the tavern at the corner, wide-eyed for news.

Chapter Twenty

MISS GEORGIE SNEPPE

KIMBERLEY slapped his thigh with sheer exuberance of joy when he heard our story: for two pins, I think, he would have thrown his hat in the air. Instead, he took a pull at his bitter beer and set the tankard down with a bang.

"Hooray!" he almost shouted. "That's immense! First-rate!" Then sinking his voice, he shook his head knowingly. "The girl's going to split on her pal!" he said. "That's about it! Feminine habit – a way they have. She's after the boodle you hinted at. Good – good! Now let's be careful. I mustn't be seen. Look here – do what I'm going to suggest. When you meet her, propose a little lunch. Put her in a taxi, and bring her down to – let's think now, where there's a nice convenient place. I know! Bring her down to Bernardino's, in Great Portland Street. I'll be there. But remember, you're not to know me, and I shan't know you. What I want is to get a good look at the young lady. Now, you're aware of what she's after? You told her you knew somebody who would give five hundred pounds to get some information about the Lomas copy, and she asked you when the other girl was out of the room if that was really genuine, and you assured her it was? Well, what's that mean? Why, of course, that she knows something! Be careful in finding out what she knows. She'll probably want something on account. Are you prepared – "

"That's all right," said Frank. "Leave it to me."

"Just so – but don't you be quixotic and buy a pig in a poke," said Kimberley. "Be sure that she can tell you something really definite and useful. That she knows something seems certain – get it out of her. Now I'm off!"

He drank off his beer and vanished, and Frank and I glanced at the clock. We still had several minutes at our disposal.

"What do you suppose she knows?" asked Frank.

But I was wondering that myself. As Frank had done all the talking I, though I had made some show of taking notes of the conversation, had chiefly occupied myself in closely watching the two girls, but more particularly Miss Sneppe, and I had formed certain conclusions.

"Precisely what, I can't think," said I. "But I've a general notion. My impression of this young lady was that she knew that her friend was treating you to a whole series of tarradiddles!"

"Yes," said Frank, "but – how's that going to throw light on the mystery that I want to solve? I'm not going to give this girl five hundred pounds merely to hear that the other was hocussing us!"

"What she can tell, and its precise relation to what we want to find out, remains to be seen," said I. "But it'll be something if she can assure us, or prove to us, that Miss Cissie Frayne treated us to a carefully prepared fairy tale. Come on – time's up!"

We went cautiously outside the tavern – and at once caught sight of Miss Georgie Sneppe, who, neatly and demurely attired for walking, was studying something in a shop window at the corner of the street. She gave us a cautioning look as we crossed over and removed our hats.

"I don't want to talk here, nor to hang about here either," she said hurriedly. "Let's go somewhere where we can talk in quiet."

"That's it!" agreed Frank. "What about a little lunch, now?" He signed to a taxi-cab which, with its flag up, was crawling along the street, and a moment later bowed our new acquaintance into its shelter. "Tell him where to go," he muttered to me. Then, as the cab moved off he turned to Miss Sneppe with an ingratiating smile. "You'll talk all the better over a bit of something good," he said. "Got any particular fancies?"

But Miss Sneppe's thoughts were not fixed on eating and drinking. She was subjecting each of us, in turn, to a careful and critical inspection, and she took no more notice of Frank's question than of the streets we were passing through.

"I say!" she said, suddenly. "I'd like to know who I'm with, and what you two are after! You're not newspaper men, I'll bet! What are you – detectives?"

"What makes you think we aren't newspaper men?" demanded Frank.

Miss Sneppe's shrewd eyes ran over us again.

"You're a great deal too well dressed for that!" she said, knowingly. "Look like West End swells! – that's what you look like!"

"Do detectives dress like West End swells?" enquired Frank banteringly.

"Detectives do all sorts of things," declared Miss Sneppe. "They can tog themselves up to look like lords or like costermongers! I don't believe you're either detectives or newspaper men, now I look at you again – not reporters, anyway. I know two or three reporters! I've a boy who's a reporter – it was he who put that bit in the paper about Cissie's book and who came to interview her this morning before you came. But she doesn't know he's a boy of mine, and she doesn't know I told him either!"

"Oh, you told him, did you?" exclaimed Frank. "Why, now?"

"So that he could make a bit of what he calls 'copy' out of it," replied Miss Sneppe, unblushingly. "He said it would make a good story – half a column – and that'll be something in his pocket. But you – now, who are you?"

Frank gave Miss Sneppe back stare for stare.

"My dear young lady!" he said. "Let me ask you a question! What're you after?"

Miss Sneppe appeared to be somewhat taken aback. Her eyes shifted from Frank to me. But I, too, was staring at her.

"Well!" she replied. "You – you said that you knew somebody who'd cheerfully give five hundred pounds to get some information that might have to do with that copy of the old book – *Pilgrim's Progress*, isn't it – that was stolen when that American gentleman was murdered. Is it true?"

"Sure!" said Frank. "Dead sure thing! Well?"

"I read all that case in the papers," continued Miss Sneppe. "All about the book, too. I – I know something that I've thought about a good deal. If I was dead certain that I'd get that five hundred pounds you spoke of, I – I could tell certain things that are – well, very queer."

Then Frank did something that I shouldn't have done and that I thought him foolish for doing. But he'd done it before I could stop him. He was sitting opposite Miss Sneppe and he suddenly bent across the space between them and looked her hard in the eyes.

"Look here!" he said, incisively. "I'm the man that'll give the five hundred pounds I spoke of, and if you want to know whether the money's safe, I've got it, and a lot more, right here in my wallet. Like to look at it?"

"Here's Bernardini's!" I exclaimed. "Wait till we're inside." I got Miss Sneppe out of the cab and, motioning her to walk into the restaurant, gave Frank a dig in the ribs.

"Don't be an ass!" I said. "Keep your money where it is – she'll speak. You're a bit too eager!"

"My way!" he said penitently. "Say, I'll leave things to you when we come to it. But for God's sake don't lose a chance for the sake of money!"

Happening to know Bernardini's pretty well, I got my companions safely inside and, by a piece of good management into a quiet corner. And looking round I saw Kimberley, not far away. Kimberley looked me full in the face and neither winked an eyelash nor moved a lip: he was an image of unconcerned stolidity. But a moment later, as we three settled ourselves, I saw him take in Miss Sneppe at a glance.

I busied myself for the next half-hour in giving our guest as good a lunch as ever she sat down to in her life – probably a much better. She ate well and heartily, but no blandishments would induce her to touch wine. No cocktails, no wines, no spirits, was apparently her motto when business was to be done. I forbade all business, however, until we had finished eating; then, over coffee and cigars – Miss Sneppe consented to smoke a cigarette – I suggested that we should resume our talk broken off in the cab. "And it is high time I said a word or two," I remarked severely, turning myself to our guest. "Let me be plain! This gentleman, I may as well tell you, is willing to give a handsome reward – "

"He said five hundred pounds!" interrupted Miss Sneppe.

"That's the figure!" muttered Frank. "What I said, I stand by!"

"Well, five hundred pounds," I continued, "to anyone who can give him information as to the whereabouts of the copy of *The Pilgrim's Progress* which was stolen from the dead body of the late Dr. Essenheim! Now – can you?" Miss Sneppe toyed with her cigarette for a minute. Then she subjected Frank to another of the half-dozen scrutinies with which she had favoured him that morning.

"Well, I think you're to be trusted!" she said at last. "I don't think you'd let down a poor girl who's got to work for her living. You'll see me right if I tell you something? Because… I can tell something!"

"I've said it!" declared Frank. "I don't break my word to either man or woman! Let's hear it."

Miss Sneppe looked round, edged her chair nearer to the table at which we sat, and leant over it.

"Well!" she said in a low voice. "To begin with, that was all a pack of lies that Cissie Frayne told you this morning!"

Frank nodded quietly.

"Yes?" he said. "Lies, eh?"

"Well, there was a bit of truth, to be sure," admitted Miss Sneppe. "There was an old lady named Miss Henrietta Cooke. She did leave, or give Cissie some stuff and that box full of old books and magazines that you saw. But… Cissie didn't find that *Pilgrim's Progress* in it!"

"She didn't?" exclaimed Frank.

"No – but she doesn't know that I know that she didn't! Mind that!"

"How do you know that she didn't?" I enquired.

"Because I know where she got it!" replied Miss Sneppe. "That's why!"

We were getting very near something definite now, and Frank and I looked at each other, and I heard him draw a deep breath. He nodded to me.

"Well?" I said. "And – where did she get it?"

"It's a bit of a story," replied Miss Sneppe. "It's like this – Cissie and me, you know, we were trained for the ballet, and so of course, we're professional dancers. Well, we aren't always working – on the stage, I mean – and sometimes we get temporary engagements at dancing clubs. Now lately we've been a good deal at the Thespidolian, in Kilburn: it's quite a respectable place with a good class of people. And for some time Cissie's been very friendly with a man who comes there now and then – a Mr. Lennard. He – "

"Stop a bit," I said. "Mr. Lennard! Do you know his other name?"

"I don't know whether Lennard is his Christian name or his surname. Mr. Lennard – that's all the name we know him by."

"You say he comes there now and then? What's that mean? How often?"

"Oh, I've known him come two or three nights in one week and then we shouldn't see anything of him for perhaps a month. Never regularly, you know."

"What is he like, this man?"

"He's a tall, rather thin, dark fellow – perhaps about thirty or thirty-five."

"Anything remarkable about his eyes?"

"I can't say – he always wore slightly-coloured glasses."

"Well, and what about him and Cissie? Great friends, you say?"

"Oh, she's very thick with him – has been for some time. And now, if you want to know, it was he – Mr. Lennard – who gave her that old book that she took to Saddleworths. But – she doesn't know that I know that!"

"How do you know it?"

"Well, not such a long time ago, I saw Mr. Lennard give her a small parcel one night and say something to her about it as he handed it to her. When we got home she laid the parcel on the mantelpiece, and it was there next morning when I got up – I'm always up first, and I go into the parlour to make a cup of tea. I looked to see what it was – it was an old *Pilgrim's Progress*, wrapped in the front page of a newspaper called the *Yorkshire Post*."

"How do you come to remember that?" I asked. "The name of a paper – used as a mere bit of wrapping?"

"Well, I'll tell you. I noticed some advertisements of theatres on it, and I read them, and I glanced at the top of the paper to see what it was. They were Leeds theatres that were advertised."

"Well – what about the book?"

"I wrapped it up again and left it where I'd found it, and late in the morning I noticed that Cissie'd removed it. Three or four days after that she came to me one day, professing to be very excited, and said she'd found an old book in Miss Cooke's box, and she believed it was worth a lot of money. She showed it to me, and it was the book I'd seen. Then I guessed there was something secret about it, so I held my tongue. I know she was up to some dodge or other and that Lennard had a share in it. That was one reason why I told that fellow I know who's a reporter – I thought it might draw Cissie out if she saw it in the paper. She thinks somebody at Saddleworths put it in."

"Was she angry about it?" I enquired.

"I don't know – she seemed a bit upset. She said something about a secret. Perhaps she didn't want Mr. Lennard to think she'd told anybody her name. For say what she or anybody likes, she got that old book from him! And look here," concluded Miss Sneppe, earnestly, "supposing that book is the book that – "

I stopped her. She was becoming a little too eager.

"Never mind that just now," I said. "Listen! – do you know where this man Lennard lives?"

"No – I've no idea," she replied readily. "But I do know this – Cissie's going to meet him tonight, and I know where!"

Chapter Twenty-one

WITHDRAWN FROM SALE!

MISS SNEPPE accompanied this last bit of information with a knowing look which seemed to indicate that we were on the very edge of a really important disclosure: I, at any rate, felt that a few more words from her might enable us to give Kimberley, still steadily munching a few feet away, the very clue he wanted.

"Well?" asked Frank.

"She told me this morning that she was going to the theatre with Mr. Lennard tonight," continued Miss Sneppe. "He'd got stalls for two, she said."

"What theatre?" I enquired.

"Lyceum!" replied Miss Sneppe. "It's a new American crook play. Cissie likes that sort. I don't – I'm all for revue, myself. Or the pictures."

Frank and I looked at each other. We were considering what to ask, or what to do, next. For there was Kimberley to think of, and presently Kimberley would, I knew, find some way of getting a report from us.

"Will Mr. Lennard call at your lodgings for her, or is she going to meet him?" I enquired.

"Oh, she'll meet him! He never has called at our lodgings. We've never seen him, except at the dancing club," said Miss Sneppe. "She'll meet him at the theatre."

"Do you know who or what this Mr. Lennard is?" I asked.

"Lord, no! I don't know anything about him, except that he comes to the club now and then!" declared Miss Sneppe. "And, of course that he's very thick with Cissie. Sort of fellow that I don't care about, though I will say that he's fairly free with his money."

"How long has he been coming there?" I asked.

"Well, I can't say, of course," she answered. "We've been going there six months back or so, and he was there the first time we went. But it's only now and then that he comes – not regularly, you know. I don't think he's a Londoner at all."

"Why don't you think he's a Londoner?"

"Well, he doesn't talk like one – I think he comes from the North Country – talks like that. I fancy he's a commercial chap – traveller, you know, because I've heard him mention a lot of places as if he'd been in them lately."

I affected to look round about us, as if there was nothing more to say just then. Kimberley had got through the more solid stages of his lunch and was lighting a cigar; his waiter was pouring out coffee for him. I gave Frank a light kick under the table.

"Just excuse me a spell," I said, rising. "Back in a few minutes."

I walked down the centre of the restaurant, contriving to give Kimberley a wink as I passed his table. He didn't show the slightest recognition of it, but within a couple of minutes he had joined me in the street outside. We turned the corner into a side-street.

"Well?" he asked, eagerly. "Got anything?"

"A good deal, I should think," I replied.

"Listen, now, and I'll give you a résumé of it. This girl says
– "

I went on to tell him everything that we had got out of Miss Georgie Sneppe, and he listened carefully and anxiously, nodding his head appreciatively at the more important points.

"Good!" he exclaimed when I had made an end. "Very good indeed and most valuable! Now look here, Captain, listen to me! You've done excellently this morning, and we're getting on to something – without a doubt this man the girl knows as Lennard is the man we've heard so much of in connection with Lomas, and we mustn't lose the slightest chance of laying hands on him. I only hope he is going to the theatre – did you say the Lyceum? – tonight with the other girl. If he is, we'll have him safe and sure! But now this girl – the girl you've got in there. Listen! – She mustn't, under any consideration, be allowed to go back to Battlement Street. Keep her away from there at all costs! Take her to the theatre, or to the pictures, or ask her to tea at the hotel – do anything, but don't let her out of your hands. And tell Mr. Frank that he mustn't on any account give her any money until I say the word! Let her know that she'll get her reward when her information results in something good – keep it dangling before her. Now go back and do what I say, and be at the Carlton between four-thirty and five o'clock in any case, so that I can ring you up if need be. As for me, I'm going to get very busy."

"What're you going to do?" I asked.

"Well, to begin with, I'm going to put a man of mine to watch that house in Battlement Street," he answered. "That other girl must be kept under observation. As for the rest – but you do as I say, and wait at the Carlton till you hear from me."

He hailed a passing taxi-cab, and was driven off, and I went back to the restaurant and gave Frank another kick. He took it as meaning exactly what I intended he should understand – namely, that he was to leave further movements to me.

"Well!" I said, adopting a somewhat jocular tone. "Miss Sneppe's given us the pleasure of her company so far, and I think we'd like a bit more of it! What do you say if we all go to the pictures for a couple of hours and then to tea at the Carlton."

At mention of the Carlton, Miss Sneppe's eyes widened and she pursed her mouth.

"My!" she exclaimed. "That's a very swell place! Do you go there?"

"That'll be all right," I said, reassuringly. "We'll look after you."

She treated us, on that, to another critical inspection.

"I'm certain you aren't newspaper fellows," she remarked. "And he " – she pointed the tip of a finger at Frank – " he's an American! You were fishing when you came to our place this morning – I know it!"

"Well, never mind!" said I. "We'll take care of you and you'll benefit by it."

"I shall get that reward, shan't I?" she asked, eyeing us alternately. "Don't forget I'm a poor girl, earning my own living – "

"You don't look as if you lived in Poverty Street, anyhow!" I said, casting an eye over Miss Sneppe's outward show. "Quite the opposite!"

"Oh, well, one's got to look nice!" she retorted. "It doesn't do to be dowdy in my profession. But that reward – you'll see that I get it?"

"Sure!" said Frank. "Make your mind easy. Good as yours, I reckon!"

We found Miss Sneppe quite amenable as to keeping our company for the afternoon; whether she had a taste for male society or was thinking about the reward she had been promised it is unnecessary to speculate upon: it is sufficient to say that after a visit to a picture palace, where we were treated to some trenchant and amusing criticism of what we saw, we steered her round to the lounge at the Carlton for tea. And I had just sipped my first cup when a page boy came to summon me to the telephone. An excited voice came through – Heddleston!

"Hello, Mannering! Is that you – is that you, Mannering? I've rung you up twice already during the last hour. I say! Here's strange news from Saddleworths. That girl, young woman or whatever or whoever she is, has withdrawn the book!"

"Withdrawn?" I exclaimed. "From the sale?"

"From the sale, of course! This afternoon – early. What's more, she's got it!"

"Got it back in her possession?"

"Yes! I say – do you know where Kimberley is? Is he with you?"

"No! I believe he's at headquarters. I'll ring him up and get him here. Will you come?"

"Right! Get him there at once, and I'll join you. Coming straight on."

I rang up Kimberley, and to my relief got in instant touch with him. Within a quarter of an hour he and Heddleston walked into the lounge together. I left Frank and our guest and went to meet them.

"There's one thing certain," said Kimberley, after a few minutes discussion. "That girl" – pointing to Miss Sneppe – "will now have to be taken into confidence! We shall need her – she knows this man whom she calls Lennard. Come over and let us talk."

Miss Sneppe received the information she presently got with great equanimity: she was, in fact, enjoying herself hugely, and I daresay she had already conceived a romance in which she, Frank, and St. George's Hanover Square, were to play parts.

"Some people," she remarked, philosophically, when Kimberley had addressed her in a half-parental, half-judicial way – "some people would say I was playing it low-down on Cissie, but I don't think so. Cissie's done me lots of dirty tricks, especially about gentlemen that we've known, and we all like to get a bit of our own back, don't we? And besides that, I've felt all along that there was something wrong about Cissie and that old book – it's my private belief it's the very book that was described in the papers at the time of the murder of that poor American gentleman. So what do you want me to do next?" She concluded, turning knowing eyes on Kimberley. "Of course, I can see you're a detective. Just the sort one reads about in the novels, aren't you?"

"Am I?" retorted Kimberley. "And perhaps I'm not, young lady! What we want you to do at present is to stop here and amuse these two gentlemen – Captain, leave Mr. Heddleston and Mr. Frank to Miss Sneppe, and you come along with me."

I followed Kimberley into Pall Mall: he hailed a taxi-cab and bundled me in.

"Sly little baggage that!" he said. "Tell Mr. Frank to beware of her! But she'll be highly useful tonight – and perhaps before."

"Where are you going now?" I asked.

"Where? Saddleworths," he said. "I want to know all about this! Of course, this Cissie Frayne girl has taken fright!"

"Or – the man who's behind her," said I. "That's more likely!"

"Or the two of 'em," he muttered. "Well, we'll see."

We drove up to Saddleworths: the managing partner whom we had seen before received us in his private office. He looked put out and before we could say a word he went straight to the point.

"You've come in consequence of our message to Mr. Heddleston," he said. "Well – there it is! The young woman's carried off the book!"

"But why was she permitted to do so?" I asked. "You know that we'd raised the question of the ownership, and that Mr. Whiteley – "

"It's all very well!" he interrupted, spreading his hands "I know all that, and if I'd been here this wouldn't have happened. But I wasn't here! I was out at lunch, and out longer than usual. Miss Frayne came here in my absence, saw one of my junior partners, and said she wanted to look at her book. He knew, having seen her before when she first brought the book to us, that it was her property, and he knew nothing about your call here nor anything about Whiteley's inspection of it. He took the book out of the safe and handed it to her. She thereupon said that she'd changed her mind and wasn't going to offer it for sale by auction as she'd heard of an American purchaser, and without another word she marched off with it! There you are!"

"Then – it's gone!" said Kimberley. "Clean gone!"

"Of course, it's gone," assented the managing partner, peevishly. "Don't I tell you so? But you know her address – you'd better go there if you want more information. I've told you all I know. And you've got to remember that as far as we were concerned we only knew that this young woman claimed the book as her property. It may be – in spite of Whiteley's affirmation."

"What do you mean?" I asked. "Whiteley's prepared to swear – "

He interrupted me with another wave of his hands.

"That may be – I won't deny that it is – the copy of *The Pilgrim's Progress* that was shown to Whiteley by Mr. Lomas," he said. "But how do you know its history since then? Anyway, the girl's got it!"

There was no good to be got in arguing any more there, and Kimberley and I left. Kimberley seemed anxious.

"What I'm wondering," he said, "is – did my man get up there to Battlement Street before this young woman went out to come to Saddleworths? If he did, he'd follow her here and afterwards. If he didn't, and she never returned there, he'll be hanging about to no purpose. We'll get into another cab, Captain, and drive round there to inspect. If my man's hanging round I shall have to find out if he's seen anything of her; if he isn't, I shall know he's on her track. Here's a taxi – get in and I'll tell the driver exactly what to do."

The driver, following Kimberley's instructions, took us up to Camden Town and arrived at Battlement Street, drove slowly from one end to the other. By Kimberley's orders I sat well back in my corner; Kimberley examined each side of the street as we passed along.

"Not there!" he said. "That means he's followed her! That's all right! She'll not give him the slip!"

"What will your man do?" I asked.

"Track her wherever she goes!" he answered, "Just that!"

"And supposing she tried to get off by train?" I suggested. "Or in any other way?"

"Well, he'd just stop her!" he said, with a laugh. "But he'll not do that unless he's obliged. My orders to him are that he's to keep her under observation, see where she goes, and if she meets anybody; and if the latter, then to follow again until something happens that'll make him consider it necessary to 'phone me. Oh, he knows what to do, right enough, and as to sticking to her after once getting a sight of her – well he's as good as a horse-leech!"

"What do you suppose has happened?" I asked.

"What I suppose has happened, Captain, is that she's gone to meet the Lennard man!" he replied. "That chap, whoever he is, is at the back of all this, and we've got to get him. Well – that bit of stuff that we left at the Carlton will come in handy now! Any means to a good end – and any tool that will break a door open, eh?" He leaned out of the window and spoke to the driver. "Go along to the Carlton Hotel," he commanded. Then, leaning back, he laughed. "The next move is with Miss Sneppe!" he said.

Chapter Twenty-two

CRUMPLED PAPER

I WAS not sufficiently versed in detective methods to know, or ever to imagine, what particular use Miss Georgie Sneppe would be put to, and I said so, whereupon Kimberley chuckled, as if amused at my ignorance.

"Very useful, indeed, Captain, a girl of that sort!" he said. "Very useful! You can make use of her in a lot of ways. She can act as a decoy. She can play the spy game. You can use her to get information that you couldn't pick up yourself. All that's necessary is to assure her that she'll get well paid for her services and to see that she doesn't play you false. I can put this young woman to a good deal of use, and I'll tackle her myself when we get in."

He lost no time in that when we rejoined the three curiously-deserted individuals we had left at the Carlton. Marshalling us all into a corner of the lounge and telling Heddleston and Frank, in an aside, the result of our visit to Saddleworths, he turned to Miss Sneppe.

"Now, my girl!" he began, with a trace of something like fatherly authority, "I want you to make yourself useful – the more useful you make yourself, the better you'll get paid and the quicker you'll touch your money! See? Now I'm going to talk straight to you. Mr. Frank there has given you his word that you'll be well rewarded, hasn't he? Very good, but you've got to earn your reward first! Now to start with, I want to know certain things. You say you saw that book, *The Pilgrim's Progress*, handed to your friend, Miss Cissie Frayne, by a man that you know under the name of Lennard? You're sure of that?"

"Certain!" replied Miss Sneppe, promptly. "As certain as that I see you!"

"Very well! You know this man Lennard quite well by sight?"

"I not only know him by sight – I've talked to him many a time and danced with him many a time. But he's Cissie's boy, of course!"

"Cissie's boy, eh? Now what do you mean by that?"

"Well, he's – don't you understand? He's her particular friend – not mine."

"Tell me this, now! Has he ever been to see her at your lodgings – at Battlement Street?"

"Yes – once or twice."

"Anything else?"

Miss Sneppe hesitated, eyeing our observant faces.

"Oh, well!" she said at last. "She's been away weekends with him now and then."

"Do you know where?" asked Kimberley.

"No, I don't – I've never heard her say where. Except just once. She did say once that they'd spent the weekend at the Miramar."

"The Miramar Hotel?" exclaimed Kimberley. "That's a pretty swell place to go to! So this Lennard's a bit free with his money, then?"

"I should say he's plenty," replied Miss Sneppe. "He's never behind-hand in standing a bottle of champagne when he comes to the Club, anyhow!"

"Did he find Cissie with money at all – do you know that?" demanded Kimberley.

"I know he gave or sent her so much a week," said Miss Sneppe. "She couldn't have bought all the things she did if he hadn't."

"Pretty good wardrobe, eh?" suggested Kimberley, eyeing Miss Sneppe's own attire.

"Quite plenty!" assented Miss Sneppe, curtly. "Didn't come out of what she earned, neither!"

Kimberley pursed his lips and inspected Miss Sneppe once more.

"Very well!" he said. "Now then, you'll remember all I've said. You're to earn whatever it is in the way of reward that Mr. Frank is going to give you, and you're to play straight. There's no doubt whatever that Cissie Frayne and that man you know as Lennard have got that book we've been talking of and have no right to it, and I want 'em! You've got to help!"

"I – I don't want to run into any danger!" said Miss Sneppe. "I don't mind rounding on Cissie – she's done me two or three real dirty tricks, and I've always wanted to be quits with her – but she's an awful cat if it comes to it, and I should say Lennard's the sort of fellow that – – "

"That what – ?" asked Kimberley, as the girl hesitated. "What?"

"Well, I should say he'd go for anybody if it came to it!" replied Miss Sneppe. "There's something about him that's – well, frightening. And if they found out – "

"They'll find out nothing," said Kimberley. "You do just what I tell you, my girl, and you'll be as safe as houses! It's simply this: I want you to go back to your lodgings and find out if Cissie Frayne is there. If she is, you make an excuse to go out again, and you meet me – I shall be close by – and tell me so. But if she isn't, you'll find out from your landlady all you can about anything that happened since you went out this morning to meet these young gentlemen. You've got a landlady there, eh?"

"Mrs. Meechin," assented Miss Sneppe.

"Will she talk?" asked Kimberley.

"Quite enough!" replied Miss Sneppe. "No fear on that ground!"

"Very well – if Cissie's out, get all the news you can about her; and when you've got it come away and tell it to me," said Kimberley. "Now come outside and we'll get a cab and go up to Camden Town. Mr. Heddleston, I suppose you don't want to go with us? No, of course – you two young gentlemen can come – you may be useful."

Making arrangements with Heddleston whereby we could keep him informed, either at his office or at his private house, of the course of our doings, Frank and I packed ourselves into a cab with Kimberley and his newly-enlisted auxiliary and journeyed once more to the dreary streets of Camden Town. Kimberley stopped the driver at some little distance from Battlement Street, and, after giving Miss Sneppe certain final directions and admonitions, sent her off with his blessing. When she had fairly gone, he prepared to leave the cab himself; he was going, he said, to keep an eye on Mrs. Meechin's house, anyway. Frank and I left alone, looked at each other speculatively.

"Thinking – what?" he asked.

"I'm wondering who on earth this man whom that girl knows as Lennard can be!" I replied. "Who?"

"I'm not," he said, laconically. "I reckon he's Lomas."

I turned and stared at him – incredulously.

"Lomas!" I exclaimed, incredulously. "Lomas?"

"Just that – Lomas!" he replied. "Hasn't the girl told us that this fellow only comes to that dancing club now and then, and that she believed, from what she'd seen and heard of him, that he was from the country? Well, didn't we find when we were in those parts that Lomas has been in the habit – constant habit – of running up to town for a few days for some time? Putting everything together, I say – Lomas!"

"No!" I said. "I say he's the man who met Lomas at Wilmoor Junction and went with him to Harlesden Hall."

"But that man, we know, had a cast, or squint, in one eye," he objected. "And this girl said nothing about that in describing him. If this fellow she knows had such a thing, she'd have noticed it."

"No!" I persisted. "Didn't she tell us that she couldn't see his eyes, because he wore tinted glasses? It's the other man!"

"I say it's Lomas!" he growled. "Lomas – murderer and thief! If I chance across him, I'll be sore tempted to take something out of my hip-pocket that I'm carrying there!"

"For God's sake don't do that in this country!" I exclaimed. "We aren't allowed to take the law into our own hands here, you know."

"Well, that's nothing to boast of," he retorted. "There are times when it's God's own justice to take the law into your own hands, and seems to me this is one of 'em! If I'd either of those two on that moor where my uncle was murdered, guess I'd get very lively with 'em, and damn the law!"

"Leave them to Kimberley," I said. "He'll get 'em! And he'll conduct 'em carefully and watchfully to the scaffold – if what I'm beginning to suspect is true."

"What are you beginning to suspect?" he asked, half satirically.

"That they were both of 'em in it," I said. "But how – "

Kimberley came back just then.

"I reckon the kid's all right," he said as he climbed into the cab. "I watched her in, and I took a quiet look past the house. The gas is on in the front parlour, and the blinds are up, so I could see in, and I saw her and the landlady having a good jaw together – at least, the landlady was doing the chin-wagging, and the little girl was taking it all in." He rubbed his hands and chuckled. "Going quite satisfactorily, this!" he said complacently. "We'll lay hands on 'em before midnight!"

"Somewhat optimistic, aren't you?" said Frank.

"Better than t'other thing, sir," replied Kimberley. "Always take the sunny side of the street – that's my motto. You see, quite apart from what this Georgie kid can tell us when she comes back, I've got one of my cleverest men on those two, and if he doesn't give me some news of 'em before long I'll be more surprised than I ever have been! Of course, I've a notion what they're after!"

"What?" I asked.

"Well, I should say that the man – Lennard – took fright when he saw that paragraph in the paper," replied Kimberley. "We, of course, know how it came to be there, and it's a piece of good luck that this Sneppe girl was thick with the reporter chap and had the sense to know it would make a bit of good 'copy' for him. I should say that Lennard got into touch with the Cissie Frayne girl after Georgie left this morning and made her fetch the book away from Saddleworths. And in my opinion he's probably going to clear out of the country with it – tonight!"

"Where?" asked Frank.

"Oh, anywhere! Paris – Brussels – anywhere where he'll be safe for a bit. My only hope is that he's taking the girl with him. If so – "

"Here's your ambassador!" I exclaimed, interrupting him. "She's safe and sound, anyway!"

Miss Georgie Sneppe came hurrying along the side street in which we had waited. She was showing all her teeth – very white and regular – in a highly satisfied smile. Kimberley flung open the door: she bustled in and sank into the seat with a sigh.

"Well, I've got news for you!" she said, looking round our expectant faces. "Of course, Cissie wasn't there! She – "

"Wait a minute," interrupted Kimberley. He leaned out of the window and gave the driver some instructions. "Now," he said, as we moved slowly away, "take your time, my dear – and begin at the beginning!"

"Well, there's plenty to tell!" said Miss Sneppe. "And if I'm to begin at the beginning, I suppose that'll be about what happened after I went out this morning. I got it all out of Mrs. Meechin – she was ready enough to talk. Mrs. Meechin says that not so very long after I'd gone, that fellow Lennard came, and – "

"Stop a bit," interrupted Kimberley. "Does Mrs. Meechin know him as Lennard? Know him by that name?"

"No!" replied Miss Sneppe. "She only knows him as Cissie's gentleman; you see, he's only been to the house once or twice before. Well, he came, and Mrs. Meechin says that after he came she heard him talking in our sitting-room as if he was very angry about something. She doesn't think they were having words, she says, because she didn't hear Cissie answering back, which is a wonder, for Cissie's got a tongue on her if she likes to let it go! It wasn't like a quarrel, Mrs. Meechin says, but as if – well, as if he was just jolly well mad about something."

"Paragraph in the papers, of course," muttered Kimberley. "Well?"

"Well, soon after that, Cissie got dressed and went out. Lennard stopped there, in our sitting-room; he got Mrs. Meechin to make him a cup of tea. Mrs. Meechin told me that he was fidgety – walked up and down with his hands in his pockets, and so on. Cissie was away a good hour or so; at last she came back, in a taxi. Mrs. Meechin says that she heard a word or two between them when Cissie opened the parlour door and walked in on him. She heard him say 'Have you got it?' and Cissie said 'Yes – all right – it's here.' Then Cissie shut the door and Mrs. Meechin heard nothing further."

"That would be the P.P." muttered Kimberley. "Go on, Kiddie."

"Well, there's not much more. They stopped in the sitting-room a bit, and then Mrs. Meechin heard Cissie go into her room. She was there some time, and when she came out she'd got her suitcase, and she told Mrs. Meechin that she was going away for a day or two and she could tell me that when I came in. Then she and Lennard went away – "

"Did she say what time they left?" asked Kimberley.

"Yes – she made them a cup of tea before they went. It was about four o'clock. Of course, she'd no idea where they went. But –" here Miss Sneppe beamed on us with an air of conscious triumph – "I've made a discovery! You can call it accidental if you like, but I did make it. Look here," she went on, opening the vanity bag, which formed a prominent feature of her equipment, and extracting what looked like a lump of crumpled pink paper, "I found this, thrown away in the fender. It's a telegram, and of course Lennard had thrown it there. Read it!"

We all read it, one after the other.

Lennard, Russel Hotel.

Seen par in paper see girl immediately make her withdraw book from sale and bring it away see you tonight at usual time and place.

"What do you make of that?" asked Miss Sneppe archly. "Ain't I cute? Is it any good?"

But Kimberley made no reply to her question beyond nodding his head and putting the telegram in his pocket. Our cab was just drawing up at the Carlton, and as we all turned towards the door a man came forward and drew Kimberley aside. They talked earnestly together for a moment; then Kimberley beckoned to me. His big face wore an expression of satisfaction and relief.

"Hooray, Captain!" he whispered. "My man – the man I put on to watch – has got 'em – at least he's run 'em to earth. They're safe enough – they're being watched closely just now. Now listen – keep this girl with you; don't let her go, for anything – give her some dinner, do anything with her except tell her what I've told you, and wait here till I ring you up!"

Chapter Twenty-three

WHAT DOES THIS MEAN?

KIMBERLEY re-entered the cab we had just quitted, and we, once more faced with the by-this-time somewhat wearisome task of acting as custodians of Miss Sneppe, ushered her again into the hotel. But there was something wholly unexpected awaiting us there – in the shape of Calvert!

Calvert stood just within the lounge, talking to Heddleston. Heddleston had the air of a man who is thoroughly perplexed; Calvert looked as if he had been worrying all the wits he possessed for an indefinite period and was still as far off as ever from any solution. At sight of us he started forward, beckoning. But Heddleston got in the first word.

"Where's Kimberley?" he exclaimed. "We want him! I've been ringing him up from the office, and they didn't know –"

"Kimberley's just left us and gone back there," I said. Then, drawing him aside, I whispered, "Kimberley's got news of the man we want! His men have him and the other girl under observation: Kimberley's going to ring us up, here, presently. What's Calvert doing here – what is it?"

"Calvert!" he said. "Calvert made a most extraordinary discovery! We ought to have Kimberley here at once – here, come across to that corner."

"The girl?" I asked, nodding in Miss Sneppe's direction. "We're not to lose sight of her until – "

"Oh, it doesn't matter!" he answered, impatiently. "She can hear it – it'll be in all the papers tomorrow morning, if it isn't in some tonight. Come aside, Calvert, and tell them all about it."

We all went over to an unoccupied corner of the lounge, grouping ourselves around Calvert, who still wore his air of struggle with a perplexing problem. He shook his head as he began to speak.

"Blessed if I know how I'm going to make things clear to you!" he said. "As for me, I can't make matters out at all, though I expect there's some explanation of 'em to be found somewhere. Well, it's just this, to begin at the beginning. Yesterday afternoon, about three o'clock, a couple of men came to me at our police-station. One of 'em was George Mitchison. George is a keeper on the Harlesden Hall estate – he's employed by the gentleman who bought the place recently, you know, from Mr. Lomas. The other was a man I know well enough by sight – Thomas Burt, a shepherd. They'd a queer tale to tell. They'd met near Harlesden Scar. Mitchison had a couple of dogs with him. While he and Burt were talking these dogs were running about. One of 'em got nosing round the crevices and holes in the rocks, and got excited about a place where he'd begun scratching. He began to whine, and then to howl, and finally to kick up such a row that Mitchison went over to see what he was after. The dog by that time had torn away a lot of soil, at the entrance to a deep crevice, and the first thing Mitchison saw was a man's foot!"

Miss Sneppe, whose eyes had been getting wider and her lips more and more parted, let out a stifled cry. But the rest of us remained stonily silent, and Calvert, after a glance at his female witness, went on.

"Mitchison noticed one thing about that foot at once! It was in a boot, to be sure, but the boot was cracked and worn, and there was no stocking. And, according to his account, he there and then said to Burt that the body was that of a tramp! Bear that in mind, in view of what you're going to hear. Well, the two men set to work – with their hands and with a crook that Burt was carrying. And before long they'd uncovered the other foot – same thing as regards its foot-wear, broken boot and no stocking – and from that they went on till they'd unearthed the whole body. It had only been lightly covered with soil, and peat, mixed with heather, torn up from close by. And underneath it – mark this – they found a heavy stick – walking-stick! Not the sort of stick you find in shops, you know, but a home-made article: a piece of stout thick oak, cut from a tree and fashioned for walking purposes with a clasp knife. Keep that stick in mind, too!"

Calvert paused for a moment – as a barrister might pause who, in his address to a jury, marks a strong point and interrupts his own eloquence while the significance of the point strikes into the minds of his listeners. Then he went on – sinking his voice, as if the more impressive things were still to come.

"They then set off to tell me. On the way they met that chap Chaffin and another man who were crossing the moor from Kirkenmore to Rievesley, and they told them what they had found, and asked them to go and watch over the body till they returned with the police. As soon as I heard this story, I got some of my men, bundled them into a car, got into my own with Burt and Mitchison, and hurried off to Harlesden Scar. Chaffin and the other man – a Rievesley chap, named Thorp, a labourer – were there when we arrived. They'd simply kept watch; nobody, Mitchison assured me, had touched the body since he and Burt discovered it – they hadn't even touched it themselves, nor interfered with it in any way except to draw the stick from beneath it – the stick, they said, had protruded a little to one side, so they had drawn it out. Well, of course, I examined the body."

He paused again there, making a face; Miss Sneppe, in sympathy, made one, too.

"Not a pleasant job, I can assure you!" continued Calvert. "But – it had to be done, and we did it. Well, it was that of a tall, spare man, a dark, not over prepossessing sort of chap, of, I should say, thirty-five to forty years of age, who was obviously of the tramp class, or, perhaps, if not a regular, what I call professional tramp, he was a man out of work for some time. It was very badly dressed, of course. As I told you at the beginning, the man had no stockings, and the boots were broken and dilapidated generally. There was a shirt and a neck-cloth, but there was no waistcoat; the jacket and trousers were much worn and of poor quality. A man utterly down on his luck! That was evident. And – here came in the thing that made me begin to see there was more in this discovery than I'd anticipated – on the right temple, and down the side of the cheek and jaw, there was what I felt sure was dried blood! There'd been a blow there! And I remembered that the doctors had said that it was just such a blow as that that had killed Dr. Essenheim!"

Somebody – perhaps it was myself – drew a deep breath. Calvert nodded.

"Yes!" he said. "Just so! Well, as soon as I saw that, I sent off a man post haste for the Kirkenmore doctors: I determined I wouldn't have the body moved until they'd seen it. We covered it up, and stood around discussing matters. Mitchison and Burt were still there, of course, and so were Chaffin and Thorp. And all of a sudden Chaffin pointed to the stick, which we had laid aside on the heather. 'That's Mr. Lomas' stick!' he said. 'I know it well enough – I cut it for him myself in our plantation year before last.' You may be sure I pricked up my ears at that. 'Are you sure of that, Chaffin?' I asked, as I picked up the stick. 'One oak stick's pretty much like another, you know.' I'm as certain on it as I am that I see you, master,' he answered. 'I fettled (made) it myself, and put a strong ferrule on it, and what's more, if you look at it careful, you'll see that I cut his initials on it – there they are. H.L.' And to be sure, he was right – the initials were there, rudely cut."

Calvert glanced round our ring of expectant faces, as if to see what impression this announcement made, and to invite comment. But we were all either too much excited or too much amazed to speak, and he presently went on with his story.

"Well, I kept the stick in my hand after that," he said. "I began to see that it was going to form a most important piece of evidence. Lomas' walking-stick – found there, under this unknown man's dead body. I asked Chaffin a question or two about it – where he had seen it last, and so on. Chaffin said he couldn't remember that – what he knew was that Lomas kept it, with other sticks, in a corner of that little untidy room in which we found the trench-coat, you remember? – it was always there, said Chaffin, except when Lomas was using it. Then, as we were talking about it, the doctors came. I got them to make a first examination of the body. They preferred, however, to defer any particular examination until it had been removed, but they said at once that there had been a violent blow on the head, and that it had probably been caused by the stick I showed them. We removed the body then to the mortuary at Kirkenmore, and the doctors proceeded to examine it carefully. And," said Calvert, with a significant shake of the head, "in my opinion the conclusions they came to, after a very exhaustive examination, are very important – considering what we know already about the case of Dr. Essenheim!"

"What are they?" asked Heddleston.

"Well, you must remember, to begin with, that the hole or crevice in which this man's body was found is at the foot of the Scar," replied Calvert. "Now according to the doctors he neither fell over the top of the Scar nor was thrown over! The only wound on him was that I'd noticed on his right temple. That, they said, was quite sufficient to cause death – instantaneous death. A real savage blow – from some blunt instrument, such as the walking-stick found beneath the body. There wasn't a broken bone – not even a little finger. It was that blow! And the man couldn't have inflicted it himself."

"Could the injury have been caused by a fall over the edge of the Scar?" asked Heddleston.

"The doctors say not – there'd have been other injuries," replied Calvert. "No, they're positive on the point I've mentioned. They gave it as their decided opinion that the man was killed by a blow on the head, and that it was caused by some such weapon as that I showed them – the Lomas walking-stick. So, having ascertained that much, the next thing was to try to find out something about the man – as to who he was, and so on. As I've already said, he was obviously of the tramp or out-of-work class; all he had on him, when we searched his clothing, was a copper or two. Now we have no workhouse, and therefore no casual ward, at Kirkenmore. But there's one at Rievesley. I thought I might get some information about this man there, so I telephoned to the Master to come over and to bring with him the official who looks after the casual ward. They came, latish last night, and they identified the man."

"As what – whom?" asked Heddleston.

"As a tramp who spent a night in the casual ward at Rievesley Workhouse some little time ago – as nearly as the man in charge of the Casuals could recollect, about the end of October. I tried to get him to be precise about the date, and I came to the conclusion, on piecing things together, that it was the night of October 21st. That was the night preceding the murder of Dr. Essenheim, of course."

There was a brief silence after this. Miss Georgina Sneppe sat regarding the Superintendent with fascinated eyes; tales of horror, evidently, had their charms for her. As for the rest of us, we were thinking, and no doubt all thinking the same thoughts. Frank probably voiced them.

"What's your theory, Calvert?" he asked.

Calvert made a gesture which seemed to signalise his bewilderment.

"I don't know!" he said frankly. "I've thought this, and I've thought that – and I don't know what to think! That is, what to think exactly. But I'm certain of one thing – this has something to do with the Dr. Essenheim affair! If we could reconstruct the whole thing – but that's impossible. You see – that stick! It's Lomas' stick, beyond a question. Was it stolen from Lomas' house? Was it – "

"More likely taken from Lomas' house by the man who struck down the tramp!" growled Frank. "And that's the man who'd already struck down my uncle! God – can't you see the whole thing, you fellows? One of those devils, Lennard or Lomas, followed my uncle with that oak stick, murdered him, and was doubtless busy robbing him when this tramp chap, making his way across the moors, came up and interrupted! So – he paid for it with his life! Double murder!"

"It might be like that," assented Calvert. "But there's nobody can tell the exact truth of that except either Lennard or Lomas, and so far – though, of course, you know more than I do about Lennard, for up to now, beyond your mere mention of his name, I know very little except what Mr. Heddleston's told me this afternoon – so far, I say, they've eluded all pursuit. What is certain is that this tramp was killed by a savage blow on the head, and that everything seems to show that he got it on the same night that Dr. Essenheim was killed in the same way. Now – "

A page-boy came along at that moment enquiring for me.

"Wanted on the telephone, sir," he announced. "That'll be Kimberley," I said, hurrying off. "Wait till I hear what he says."

Kimberley's voice sounded calm, cool: he was evidently well pleased with things.

"That you, Captain?" he said. "Listen! All's going excellently. We know where they are, all safely fixed, as they fondly believe, for the night, and we've got 'em under observation. They can't possibly escape us. So now, get Mr. Frank to look after the little girl, and you come along to meet me at – "

"Stop a bit, Kimberley!" I said. "Here's a new development. Heddleston's here with Calvert, who has hurried up from Kirkenmore with some startling news which you ought to hear at once. It's astonishing news!"

"Then bring Calvert with you," he answered. "Make Heddleston take charge of the Sneppe girl – she mustn't be allowed out of sight till we've done with her – and you and Mr. Frank and Calvert come along and meet me. What's Calvert's story?"

"Can't tell you over the 'phone," I answered. "Too long. But it's most important."

"Come on, then," he replied. "Come at once – I'll start too. Where? Oh, didn't I say? Come to the bookstall – principal one – at Victoria Station. You'll find me hanging round. Yes – just now!"

I went back to collect Frank and Calvert. And as I went the impression grew strong on me that we were approaching the last act of the drama.

Chapter Twenty-four

TRAPPED!

WE left Heddleston – not at all to his liking – in charge of Miss Sneppe, and, putting Calvert into a cab, went off with him to Victoria, giving him on the way an account of the afternoon's developments, so that he might be well posted by the time we met Kimberley.

"This is a queer case, gentlemen!" he said when he had heard everything. "The finding of this tramp's body complicates it, in my opinion. There are things, you see, which, so far as I can forecast matters, never can be explained! More's the pity!"

"Such as what, Calvert?" I asked.

"Well, did that tramp follow Dr. Essenheim across the moors, purposely?" he answered. "He may have done, you know. It's odd that he should have been there, at Harlesden Scar, just about the time that Dr. Essenheim was murdered. It might be argued – perhaps will be – that he followed Dr. Essenheim first to Harlesden Hall, waited till he left there, and then dogged his path till they got to the Scar."

"And – then?" said Frank.

"These others – Lomas and the unknown man, whose name, you say, is Lennard, may say that the tramp killed Dr. Essenheim," replied Calvert. "It's likely!"

"Who killed the tramp, then?" I asked.

Calvert shook his head.

"Aye!" he answered with a sigh. "Just so, Captain! But these fellows – and you're only expecting to lay hands on one of them – are in a tight hole, and they'll snatch at anything. Their explanation may be that they found the tramp and Dr. Essenheim engaged in a tussle, joined in, and settled the tramp just after he'd settled Dr. Essenheim! That they've got the book – that they're in unlawful possession of it – there's no doubt, and there's no doubt, either, as to how and when they got it. But what I want to see is a definite conviction, and after all where's our evidence to prove the actual identity of Dr. Essenheim's murderer?"

"The stick!" I said. "Lomas' stick!"

"I know – I know!" he assented. "Splendid bit of evidence, that stick – if we could only prove that it was in that little room of Lomas' when Dr. Essenheim called there! But Chaffin couldn't swear to that – all he can say is that it was always kept there. Well, if Kimberley's going to collar this Lennard man tonight, we'll likely hear more before tomorrow. But mark my words – this chap, whoever he is, will throw all the blame on Lomas! And – where is Lomas? Gone – clean gone!"

"We don't know that, Calvert," said I. "London is an excellent place to hide in. Lomas may be nearer than you think. Who was it that wired to this man Lennard at the Russell Hotel this morning? In my opinion, Lomas!"

Frank made a growl of assent at that, but Calvert showed his doubt by another shake of his head.

"From all I've known of him," he observed, "I can't conceive of Lomas taking a leading part in anything. Country bumpkin – that's how I've always regarded Lomas. I don't think that Lomas would take fright at seeing that paragraph in the paper this morning, nor that he's sufficiently intelligent to see that publicity would be fatal to whatever plans had been made about selling the book by auction. No! What I think is that the telegram to Lennard was from some man, perhaps a dealer who was in the secret. Lomas! No, I'll lay anything Lomas is well out of the country. Still – Kimberley's got this other chap – or we'll hope he's going to get him. Where do you say he's tracked him and the girl to?"

"The Grosvenor Hotel," I answered.

"I've stayed there once or twice," remarked Calvert, "on my way to France. Big and busy place that! Crowds of folk who just come in from the Continental trains, or are waiting for 'em – Kimberley'll have to mind they don't give him the slip. Why, they can accommodate hundreds of guests there – more like a fair sometimes, from what I've seen. Risky business I should call it, having two suspects in that place. However, I reckon Kimberley knows his business."

Kimberley, suddenly appearing from nowhere as we hung about the bookstall at Victoria, looked, not only as if he knew his business, but was highly satisfied with the way he and his assistants were conducting it. He drew us aside, and we told him, as briefly as possible, the news which Calvert had brought to town. To my surprise, it seemed to give him very little astonishment. He reflected on it for a moment, and then turned to the immediate subject.

"Well, that's a queer tale, Calvert," he said "and it'll have to be gone into thoroughly. But now, the thing is to get these two – Lennard, as we know him, and the Frayne girl. Let me tell you my arrangements – what we've done, and what we're going to do. My man – the man I had watching Battlement Street – tracked these two easily this afternoon. They went away from the girl's lodgings in a cab, and drove straight to the Grosvenor Hotel here," – he turned, pointing to that wing of the hotel which overlooks the interior of the station – "and there they booked a room under the names of Mr. and Mrs. Lambert: my man, who's up to every dodge you can think of, promptly booked another, and so got a good look at the Lennard chap's signature in the register. Naturally, he kept his eye on them once they'd entered the hotel, but he now did another thing: he communicated with me by telephone, and in consequence of what he said I sent another man to help him. Now for a sequence of events. Mr. and Mrs. Lambert, after spending some little time in their room, came down into the drawing-room and had tea: my two men had tea close by them. Mr. Lambert had brought down with him a small suitcase – really, I suppose, a sort of attaché case, and as soon as he and his lady had finished tea he strolled out with it, followed by one of my men. He went out by the sidedoor into the station – that door that you see there – and approached the left-luggage office. There he deposited his little case, and put the ticket, in his pocket. I propose to know what there is in that case before the evening's over! He then bought some papers and magazines at the hotel and returned to the drawing-room, where he and the girl settled down to reading. One of my men therefore went back to headquarters and reported to me. As a consequence, I sent him back, and a little later I sent two other men – in evening dress – with instructions, after they'd had the two wanted pointed out to them, to dine there and keep an eye on them during dinner. You see, Calvert, I wasn't going to lose any chances! The critical moment, I felt sure, was at hand. Well, things went on all right – Mr. and Mrs. Lambert never left the hotel, and my little army had 'em under constant observation. So it moved until near dinner-time; they went up to their room a bit before and came back (their bedroom door had been watched the whole time) for dinner suitably togged up – he in a dinner jacket and she in a smart gown, and in they went. So did my two swells – chaps that I pick out now and then for this sort of thing – and sat close to 'em! After dinner they went into the upstairs lounge and had coffee – so did my watch-dogs. And eventually I came on the scene – one of the crowd, eh? – and got my reports. And the situation is this: Not long before I appeared, Lambert, or Lennard, or what the devil the fellow's name is, went to the theatre-ticket office in the hotel hall, and after some enquiry booked three stalls for the Pyrstheum Theatre – my principal man was close by when he booked 'em. Three mind you: three, not two! Well, the show at that spot doesn't begin till 9.15; it's now 8.45. I've just been into the hotel for the last look before operating: and what's more, I've had a private interview with the manager and given him a hint and promised him to carry the thing out as quietly as possible. Now I'll tell you precisely what to do. I want you and Mr. Frank, Captain, to see, but not to be seen. I've my four men all ready in the hotel; the two men who are posing as swells are in the lounge; the other two are in the hall. Calvert, you and I'll make six – you come in with me. You other two gentlemen go round to the principal entrance of the hotel in Buckingham Palace Road – just round the corner of the station – and look out. And, when they come out to go to the theatre, I shall take 'em!"

Frank suddenly laid a hand on Kimberley's arm.

"You're making a mistake!" he said. "That third theatre ticket? That's for somebody who'll meet 'em there. It may be the other man – Lomas!"

Kimberley started – and hesitated.

"Um!" he muttered. "Might be! Well, we could follow them and take 'em there – at the theatre – but – "

At our elbows Calvert suddenly let out a smothered exclamation. He started back, behind the rest of us.

"Good Lord!" he said, stifling his voice. "There is Lomas!"

We all looked round in the direction he indicated. And there, true enough, not a dozen yards from us, was Lomas! He was striding across the station, looking neither to right nor left, hurrying towards the platform door of the hotel; in another second or two he had disappeared within it.

"That's Lomas," repeated Calvert. "You saw him?"

"I saw him," I assented. "Lomas, certainly! Did you see him, Kimberley – will you know him?"

For I knew that Kimberley had never seen Lomas before, and Lomas, a light overcoat thrown loose over his dinner clothes, was pretty much of a muchness with hundreds of other ordinary respectable-looking citizens.

"I shall know him!" said Kimberley. "So that's Lomas? All right – now we shall get all three, together. Go round to the front entrance, you two young gentlemen, Calvert, come with me!"

The two men went into the hotel, and Frank and I, silent, walked round into Buckingham Palace Road and to the hotel's main entrance. The full flood of traffic was going on there; cars, cabs, omnibuses passing and repassing in a never-ceasing stream. Now and then the hotel porters hailed a cab for guests; now and then cars and cabs drew up, depositing guests and their luggage. We waited ten, fifteen, twenty minutes, hanging around . . .

Suddenly a hotel porter ran down the steps; darted across the road; came back with three cabs from a neighbouring rank. Then, quicker than I can set it down, what appeared as a little procession of men and one woman came quickly out of the swinging doors, down the steps, across the pavement, sorting itself into the cabs. The cabs drove off... we turned, open-mouthed, to find Kimberley at our side, rubbing his hands.

"Worked like a well-oiled machine, gentlemen!" he purred. "Smooth as a summer sea! They hadn't a cat's chance once it came to it. But they were both – look there!"

He drew a hand from the pocket of his overcoat and showed us a couple of revolvers.

"They might ha' used those – if they'd had the opportunity," he remarked. "But they had none! Now come round to that left-luggage office – I'm going to see what's in the little case."

Chapter Twenty-five

THE WALKING-STICK

WE had been so much impressed by the swiftness and neatness with which the three suspects had been hurried out of the hotel and driven away that for a minute or two we followed Kimberley in a sort of wondering silence. Then, as we turned into the station, Frank found his tongue.

"Did they say anything – let out anything?" he asked.

Kimberley laughed.

"Let out?" he said, chuckling. "Well, the girl let out a bit of a scream – as a preliminary to a flood of abuse of the two men for getting her into a hole. I should say they'd made a cats-paw of her, though, of course, she told you two gentlemen a pack of lies – put up to it, no doubt. No! There wasn't much said. Lomas wanted to jaw and to argue: the other chap shut him up. He, that second chap, was a bit impudent and defiant. He didn't know two things that I knew. One that he'd been seen to deposit that little case we're now going to get. The other, that – though I said nothing, I'd seen him before."

"Where?" I asked.

"In the Dock, at the Old Bailey – Central Criminal Court, you know – two or three years ago," replied Kimberley. "Oh, I knew him again!"

"What was that for?" inquired Frank.

"Turf frauds! Bilking bookmakers. As far as I remember, there'd been a conviction or two before. Bad lot, evidently. He began to sing small, however, when I took this receipt for his little suitcase out of his waistcoat pocket. Up to then he'd been, as I said, defiant. You see, we'd searched his luggage – just a portmanteau – and the girl's, and found nothing. But I'll lay anything we find something in the case I'm now going to get. Look here – go into that waiting-room and I'll come back with it."

He rejoined us in a few minutes and set down on the waiting-room table a small brown leather attaché case on which, in black letters, were stamped the initials C. L. It was locked, but the locks on such articles are of a simple and flimsy sort, and within a minute Kimberley had lifted the lid. In another he had withdrawn from amongst a miscellaneous collection of toilet articles – socks, handkerchiefs, and the like – two small parcels wrapped in newspaper. And in a third there lay before us the shabby little *Pilgrim's Progress*, in its original half-sheepskin binding, and side by side with it, Miss Audrey Varnam's *Book of Hours!*

• • • • •

We left Kimberley a few minutes later, and returned to our hotel – to relieve Heddleston and dismiss Miss Georgina Sneppe, who, I may as well say, departed in a state of high satisfaction and with a wad of banknotes carefully concealed about her small person. Heddleston, of course, remained to hear all we had to tell him, and while he was there Calvert joined us, and there was much speculation as to what would be the outcome of it all. But early next morning we got further than speculation. Kimberley walked in on us soon after breakfast, and, dropping into a chair, produced some folded sheets of paper from his pocket.

"Lomas," he announced, "has made a statement. What some people would call a clean breast. I thought he would, last night. And he didn't lose much time about it either! Just after Calvert had left us, Lomas sent for me and said he wanted to tell all he knew – the game was up. I warned him in the usual fashion – you know – but he persisted. So I got a man to take down all he said, had it read over to him when he'd finished, let him correct and initial an alteration or two, and after warning him again, let him sign it. Here it is – I'll read it to you. Whether it's all strictly true or not, God only knows! But if it's all strictly true – and it may be, every word of it – it still leaves unanswered the question – who killed Dr. Essenheim?"

"Why!" exclaimed Frank, "Doesn't Lomas know?"

"He doesn't!" replied Kimberley. "There's only one man in the world who knows that! The other fellow! And I don't believe he'll ever open his lips – unless he does so when he's on trial. But the real secret is with him! However, listen to what Lomas says."

He unfolded his papers and began to read:

'This is a voluntary statement made by me, Hird Lomas, formerly of Harlesden Hall, near Kirkenmore, Yorkshire, I having been duly warned before making it that any information I hereby give may be used against me. I wish to say at once that I did not kill Dr. Charles Essenheim and that I do not know who did. I desire to say all I know about this matter from the time of my discovery of my copy of *The Pilgrim's Progress* in my house. After finding it, I showed it to Mr. Whiteley, the bookseller, of York. He advised me to

offer it to Dr. Charles Essenheim, of New York, as a man likely
to give the best price for it. I wrote to Dr. Essenheim. He
replied that he was shortly coming to England and would
communicate further with me. During the time that intervened between my showing the book to Whiteley and Dr.
Essenheim's coming to London I had a transaction with the
book. I was hard up: I wanted ready money very badly. I
knew a man who had money: he was known to me as Charles
Lambert. I believe his real name is Charles Lambie, but he
also goes under the name of Lennard. I used to meet him
occasionally at race-meetings in various parts of the country.
I don't know what he is: I never have known, but I believe
he has something to do with the Turf, and also that he lends
money: he had lent me money, at interest, more than once,
which had been repaid. I met Lambert soon after seeing
Whiteley, and told him about my find, and mentioned that
I wished I could raise some money on it there and then. He
saw the book, made some inquiries of his own about it, and
then offered to buy a half-share in it for five hundred pounds
cash down. There were conditions. First, he was to hold the
book until Dr. Essenheim came. Second, I was to advise Dr.
Essenheim that a friend of mine had equal shares in the book.
Third, he, Lambert, was to be present when Dr. Essenheim
inspected the book. I agreed to all this, and he paid me the
money – £500.

'Dr. Essenheim came to England and I got in
communication with him at his club in London and we
settled that he was to call at my house, Harlesden Hall, early
in the evening of Tuesday, October 22nd. I let Lambert know
of this arrangement. He was then in Leeds on some business,
and we arranged that he should come to Wilmoor Junction
that day – Tuesday, October 22nd – and that I should meet
him there. I did so. He turned up without a coat, saying
something about never wearing one till the weather grew

really cold. It was cold enough up there that afternoon, and I lent him an old trench-coat of mine that I had in my car. I may mention, though you won't see the importance of it at present, that this trench-coat had a hole in one of the outside pockets.

'I drove Lambert home to Harlesden Hall, and soon after we'd got there a man from London, an estate agent, came to see me about selling the place. He was not long there, but I believe he saw Lambert standing in the hall or passing from one room to another. My man Chaffin never saw Lambert there at all.

'Soon after the estate agent had gone – he was not there very long – Dr. Essenheirn came. Lambert was introduced by me to Dr. Essenheim as the friend who owned a half-share in the book. Dr. Essenheim was not long in doing business. He offered us £5,000 spot cash. We accepted it, and he at once paid the money in Bank of England notes. I offered him a drink, – whisky and soda. We all had a drink, and smoked Dr. Essenheim's cigars. He stayed a while chatting. It was all about books – rare books and their prices. He showed us a sort of prayer-book which he'd got that day in the neighbourhood, he said, but he wouldn't, or didn't, tell us who from. He said it was worth at least £8,000 or £9,000. He also showed us some curiosities he had in his pocket, amongst them an Indian arrow-head, mounted in gold, which he said had a family history. He was very friendly and chatty, and before leaving begged me to have another look round the house with a view to finding some more old stuff. When he left he told us he was going to stay the night at Kirkenmore and go on next morning to York. I went down to the gates with him, and put him on to the path leading to Kirkenmore by way of Harlesden Scar, and I warned him to be careful about crossing the top of the Scar. It was, of course, dark then, but what we should call a clear night up there, with a good deal of frost in the air and plenty of stars.

'When I got back to the house and rejoined Lambert, one of us, I forget which, suddenly saw the gold-mounted arrow-head lying on the table. Lambert said he'd run after Dr. Essenheim with it: if he didn't catch him up he'd go on with it to the hotel at Kirkenmore. He put on my old trenchcoat again, seized a stick of mine which stood in a corner, and set off. Not long after he'd gone, my man Chaffin came in: he'd been out marketing. I didn't say anything to him about Lambert: Chaffin lived in the new part of the house. I suppose Chaffin went to bed soon after that – anyway, Chaffin never knew anything about what happened that night.

'I expected Lambert back very soon, but quite an hour passed before he came. Then I saw him running up the drive. He was panting for breath when he got in, and I noticed that he hadn't brought back the stick he'd taken away. He said at once that a nice thing had happened, and swallowed some neat whisky before he could say any more. Then he said that he went as hard as he could after Dr. Essenheim, but hadn't caught him up by the time he came to the rise up Harlesden Scar. As he made up that, he heard sounds of scuffling or a fight at the top of the rocks. He rushed up and saw two men there, who appeared to be struggling together. They came apart, then he heard a sharp cry and saw one man stagger and fall. He ran forward; the man who had struck down the fallen man turned on him with some weapon. Lambert struck at him as he came on, and hit him over the head, and the man threw up his arms and fell forward on his face.

'Lambert went on to say that as soon as he'd got his breath, he struck a match and looked at the man he'd knocked down. He was dead. He then went and looked at the other man. He was dead, too, and Lambert saw that it was

Dr. Essenheim. He then returned to the man he, Lambert, had killed, and saw from his general appearance that he was a tramp. He immediately concluded that this man had followed Dr. Essenheim from Rievesley to Harlesden Hall and had attacked him, in order to rob him, at the top of Harlesden Scar.

'After making certain that both men were dead, Lambert set off back to me. On his way back he discovered that he had lost the arrow-head: it had slipped through the hole in the pocket of the trench-coat. It was, of course, too dark to look for it: he came on to my house, and told me what I have just told you. We went back to Harlesden Scar at once.

'I wish to tell the plain truth about what next happened, without any excuses for myself. I declare, however, that the suggestions as to what we were to do came from Lambert. He had got over his fright, or his nerves, by that time. He reminded me that Dr. Essenheim had on him *The Pilgrim's Progress* for which he had just given £5,000, and was, no doubt, worth at least a couple of thousand more, and the other book which he had told us was worth at least £8,000 or £9,000. Lambert proposed that we should take these, drop Dr. Essenheim's body over the rocks, and if it was found, leave it to be supposed that he had fallen over the edge in trying to find his way to Kirkenmore. As to the other man, obviously a tramp, we could easily get rid of him, and probably nobody would ever make any enquiry concerning him.

'We carried this out. We took everything from Dr. Essenheim that his pockets held, and dropped the body over the rocks. We then took the tramp's body down the side and pushed it into a crevice – Lambert put under it my stick – and covered it up with earth, turf, and heather. This done, we returned to Harlesden Hall, and a little later I got out my car, lent Lambert an ulster of mine, and drove him through

225

the night to the outskirts of Leeds. After I had set him down and had arranged to meet him in London in a day or two, I returned home. After breakfast, I set off again, and after calling at the bank in Rievesley to pay in the money Dr. Essenheim had given us (for reasons of his own Lambert had taken a cheque from me for his half) I went on to London. I was in London, in close touch with Lambert, until the news of the finding of Dr. Essenheim's body came out in the papers. We consulted as to what was to be done, and finally, at his suggestion, I went down to Kirkenmore and told Calvert a story which we believed would satisfy him.

'As to what was done later about offering the book to Saddleworths for sale by auction, that was all engineered by Lambert. He assured me that he could get this young woman, Cissie Frayne, to play her part quite successfully, and he said it would be impossible for any expert to say positively that the copy she took to Saddleworths was the one we sold to Dr. Essenheim. I left it all to him. However, when I saw this morning, in the paper, that her name had come out, I wired him at once to make her take the book away, for I saw that things were becoming dangerous.

"I have told the whole truth, as far as I know it, in this statement. I don't know who killed Dr. Essenheim: I know only what Lambert told me about that. Since he first gave me his account of it, Lambert has never referred to the matter again."

Kimberley ceased reading, and, re-folding the papers, returned them to his pocket.

"That's where the thing rests, at present," he remarked. "You see, it's as I said before – we don't know who killed Dr. Essenheim! If Lambert's story is true –"

But at that Frank jumped to his feet and strode out of the room. He gave Kimberley a look as he went which made the detective turn wonderingly to me.

"What's he mean?" he asked.

"He means he's not much doubt on the subject!" I replied. "Nor have I, Kimberley! The presence of the tramp was one of those remarkable coincidences of which one does hear, now and then."

"You mean – you think Lambert killed Essenheim?" he suggested.

"You've hit it!" I answered. "I do!"

"Well," he said reflectively. "Of course, it'll be for the jury to say. And you never know how jurymen will take things."

• • • • •

The jurymen who held the fate of these three people in their hands when the next York Assizes came on made short work of Lambert, alias Lambie, alias Lennard. They found him guilty of wilful murder. Lomas' walking-stick, that bit of solid weighty oak, did it. For he carried that... but there was no evidence to show that the unfortunate tramp carried anything. And Lambert was hanged, and Lomas, acquitted on the graver charge and found guilty on less serious indictments, disappeared to penal servitude. As for Miss Cissie Frayne, she, in consideration of her youth and ignorance, and the fact that she acted, practically, under coercion, got off very lightly.

• • • • •

There is but one thing more to add to this story: Frank Essenheim was one of those young gentlemen who, having formed an opinion – on good grounds, of course – are determined to back it. Now Frank was firmly convinced that what really happened at Harlesden Scar was this – Lambert went after Dr. Essenheim with the express intention of murdering and robbing him. He had attacked and perhaps struck him down when the unlucky tramp came up. The tramp intervened. So Lambert murdered him. Therefore, Frank said, he must do something for the tramp. But the tramp was dead. So, to even matters, Frank erected a stone over his grave in Kirkenmore Churchyard. And there is an inscription on it:

> *"To the Memory of an Unknown Man*
> *Who Lost his life in Endeavouring to*
> *Save the Life of a Stranger."*

I have come to the conclusion that there is a rich vein of poetic sentiment in the mentality of the genuine American.

THE END